A Call to Battle

As he entered the square, old Lord Capulet called to his wife. "Give me my sword, dear!" he shouted. "I'll show those Montagues what's what!"

"You, calling for a sword?" she taunted. "You'd do better to call for a crutch!" But off Lord Capulet went, waving his sword wildly as he staggered toward the battle. His wife hurried after him, trying to drag him back to safety.

The bloody fighting grew so intense it was hard to imagine it would ever stop. But it did stop—suddenly. Two fighters on the edge of town saw something that made them stand still. Others around them looked up too, and stood frozen in place. Swiftly, a stillness swept across the crowd, until all stood, or sat, or lay, gazing up at a sight that sent a chill through their veins.

ROMEO & JULIET

by William Shakespeare

retold by Billy Aronson

Interior illustrations by Hokanson/Cichetti

Wishbone illustrations by Kathryn Yingling

HarperPaperbacks

A Division of HarperCollins*Publishers*

HarperPaperbacks *A Division of* HarperCollins*Publishers*
10 East 53rd Street, New York, N.Y. 10022

Cover photographs by Carol Kaelson

A Creative Media Applications Production
Art Direction by Fabia Wargin Design
Project Management by Ellen Weiss
Edited by Matt Levine

First printing: May 1996

Printed in the United States of America

HarperPaperbacks and colophon are trademarks of
HarperCollins*Publishers*
WISHBONE is a trademark and service mark of
Big Feats! Entertainment

❖ 10 9 8 7 6 5

ROMEO

Introduction

All set to enter a world of action, adventure, drama, and laughs? Then come along with me, **Wishbone**. You may have seen me on my TV show. Often I am the main character and sometimes I am the sidekick, but I'm always right in the middle of a thrilling story. Now, I'm going to be your guide as we explore one of the world's greatest books — ROMEO & JULIET. Together we'll meet a lot of interesting characters and discover places we've never been! I guarantee lots of surprises too! So find a nice comfy chair, and get ready to read with **Wishbone**.

Table of Contents

William Shakespeare

Hello there, you lucky reader! It's **Wishbone** here, chomping at the bit to welcome you to the wild world of Will. Will who? Will Shakespeare, of course. William Shakespeare is thought to be the greatest playwright of all time by countless humans—and at least one terrier! In my humble opinion, this guy wrote the saddest tragedies, the funniest comedies, and the most romantic romances of all time. His plays are filled with fascinating characters and inventive language. The art of writing plays was never the same after Shakespeare!

Not much is known about Shakespeare's life. He was born in 1564 in Stratford-upon-Avon, a small town in the English countryside. In 1582, he married Anne Hathaway, the daughter of a local farmer. William and Anne had three children, but only two of them survived.

In 1588, Shakespeare went to London and began writing and producing his plays. By 1592, the guy had become a success. His plays were even performed for Queen Elizabeth I and King James I.

Most of Shakespeare's plays can be divided into three categories: histories (usually based on kings and other important people from England, Greece, and Rome), comedies, and tragedies. Shakespeare often retold other people's stories or got his plots from history texts called *chronicles*.

But Shakespeare didn't only write plays. He also wrote *sonnets*. Sonnets are special poems that are fourteen lines long. Most of Shakespeare's sonnets are about love.

Shakespeare died in 1616, but his plays and poems live on. *Romeo & Juliet* was written in the late sixteenth century. This sad tale of young love is one of the most famous and best-loved of Shakespeare's works.

You may not have had a chance to see or read any of Shakespeare's plays, but you're probably familiar with some of his words. Ever heard anyone say "Neither a borrower nor a lender be," "Something is rotten in the state of Denmark," "All the world's a stage," or "What's in a name?" These and lots of other phrases from Shakespeare's plays have become so famous that people use them every day without even realizing they were written by Shakespeare!

Seeing one of Shakespeare's plays for the first time is an unforgettable experience. From the minute the stage lights go up, you can tell you're in for a real feast—a cast of great characters, wild costumes, striking sets, and a gripping plot. But one thing might occur to you before anything else: Shakespeare's characters talk funny!

There are two reasons why Shakespeare's characters speak the way they do. One is that most of the time they're speaking poetry. You know how rappers use rhymes and driving rhythms to make their points with extra power? Shakespeare's characters use rhyme and rhythm to express themselves with extra power too.

The type of verse Shakespeare uses in his plays is called *iambic pentameter*. In iambic pentameter, each line of verse is broken into five parts, which are called *feet*. The last syllable of each foot is stressed, or spoken more loudly, just as certain syllables are spoken more loudly in rap.

To give you an example of how iambic pentameter works, let's look at a famous line from the play, *Romeo & Juliet*. When Romeo sees Juliet stepping out onto her balcony, he thinks her face is like the sun lighting up the night. He might have said, "Hey, wait a minute. What's that light coming through the window?" But instead, he utters a beautiful line of iambic pentameter: "But soft, what light through yonder window breaks?"

Can you divide the ten syllables of that line into five feet? If you do, it looks like this: "But soft/what light/through yon/der win/dow breaks?" Since it's iambic pentameter, the last syllable in each of the five feet is stressed. If those were the only stressed syllables, when Romeo said the line out loud, it would sound like this: "But SOFT/what LIGHT/through YON/der WIN/dow BREAKS?" Try saying the line out loud this way. Can you hear the rhythm?

But if every line had this exact same rhythm, Shakespeare's verse might get a little monotonous. So he puts in other stressed syllables besides these. If you say the line out loud, you'll see that it's more natural to say it like this: "But SOFT/WHAT LIGHT/through YON/der WIN/dow BREAKS?" So you see, by using iambic pentameter, Shakespeare can get a beat going and throw in lots of different rhythms too!

Another reason Shakespeare's characters sound different than people do nowadays is because the English language has changed a lot since Shakespeare's time. He lived four hundred years ago, in a time when people said *thee* and *thou* instead of *you*, *looketh* instead of *look*, *hast* instead of *has*, *alas* instead of *oh my*, and *Zounds!* instead of *Whoa, dude!*

But the version of *Romeo & Juliet* you're about to read isn't written in Shakespearean English. It's written in modern English, the language you use every day. This *Romeo & Juliet* is also different from Shakespeare's because it's not a play. The story is told in narrative form, like a thriller or a romance novel.

In spite of these differences, the plot and characters are pretty much the same as the plot and characters that Shakespeare made famous in his play.

Even though the book is written in modern English, you're still going to get little bits of Shakespearean English tossed in as an added bonus—courtesy of me! You see, when I get near one of Shakespeare's stories I get swept away by my love for his great words. And since this introduction is coming to a close, and I'm getting nearer and nearer to a Shakespeare story—I canst not restrain myself! I feeleth myself getting carried away! Alas, poor dog, thou looseth thy self-control!

But fear thou not, reader mine. This Shakespeare-struck dog shall not distract thee from the terrific journey that lieth ahead. Readst thou on, say I!

MAIN CHARACTERS

Romeo — a member of the Montague
  (MON-tah-gyoo) family

Juliet — a member of the Capulet
  (CAP-yoo-let) family

Lord Capulet — Juliet's father

Lady Capulet — Juliet's mother

Lord Montague — Romeo's father

Lady Montague — Romeo's mother

Friar Laurence — Romeo's friend; a priest

The Nurse — Juliet's personal servant

Benvolio (ben-VOH-lee-oh) — Romeo's friend

Tybalt (TIB-alt) — Juliet's cousin

Paris — a rich count who wants to marry Juliet

The Prince — ruler of the city of Verona

Sampson — a Capulet servant

Gregory — a Capulet servant

Peter — a Capulet servant

SETTING

Romeo & Juliet takes place in the city of Verona, Italy, and the nearby town of Mantua. The play was first performed in the late sixteenth century.

1
Feuding Families

Long ago in the town of Verona, Italy, there lived two wealthy families, the Capulets and the Montagues. These two families couldn't stand each other. No one knew why the Capulets and the Montagues hated each other so much, or how their feud began. Although no one could explain the feud, no one could stop it either. So it continued through the ages, as one generation picked up where the last had left off.

Our tale begins one hot afternoon in Verona's bustling town square, where a couple of Capulet servants were looking for trouble.

"If I spot one of those stupid, ugly Montague servants, I'll walk right up to him and pick a fight," boasted Sampson, the skinnier of the two.

"You haven't got the guts to pick anything," retorted Gregory.

This made Sampson angry. "You really don't believe I can stand up to one of those weakling Montagues?" he barked.

"I believe you could stand up to a weakling Montague. But if a strong one came along—"

"I'm talking about any Montague!" Sampson bragged. "Any stinking, slimy Montague who has the bad luck to walk within ten feet of me will be sliced into a million trillion tiny bits!"

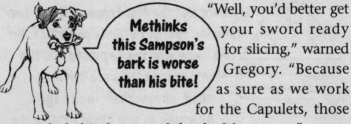

Methinks this Sampson's bark is worse than his bite!

"Well, you'd better get your sword ready for slicing," warned Gregory. "Because as sure as we work for the Capulets, those guys right behind you work for the Montagues."

Indeed, a couple of Montague servants were coming their way. "Watch me!" whispered Sampson to his friend. "I'm going to send a huge glob of spit their way!"

True to his word, as the Montague servants passed, Sampson spit onto the ground just behind them. The Montague servants stopped and looked at the spit. Then they looked up at Sampson.

"Did you spit at us?" asked one.

"I did spit," answered Sampson.

"But did you spit at *us*?" asked the second Montague servant.

"I spit where I choose to spit," was Sampson's careful reply.

"Are you trying to start a fight with us?" asked

Gregory. He wanted a fight, but didn't want to be blamed by officers of the law for starting it.

"No, we're not trying to start a fight with you," replied one Montague servant.

"But we're not trying to stop a fight either," replied the other. "Unless you Capulets are scared—which I guess you are. So we'll just be on our way." With that the Montague servants turned their backs.

"You dare to call Capulets scared?" barked a feisty Capulet named Tybalt, who came charging through the square to join Sampson and Gregory. "I hate fear, as much as I hate all Montagues and anyone from their house. You stink like horse manure!"

At this last insult the Montague servants turned around to face the Capulets: Sampson, Gregory, and Tybalt. All five stood facing one another, staring into each other's angry eyes. Each had a hand near his sword. Since the Montagues were outnumbered, they stepped back. When they noticed a Montague named Benvolio approaching, they became bold again. One of the Montagues drew his sword, and suddenly all six of them were engaged in a violent fight.

"Put down your swords, people!" shouted Benvolio. "The Prince said we've got to stop fighting in public places!"

"You're smacking your sword against my sword and talking about peace?" mocked Tybalt. "Typical Montague stupidity."

"I only took my sword out to defend myself," said Benvolio. "And I'm only smacking it against yours so you don't stab me to death!"

Although Benvolio begged the others to stop, it was too late. Already dozens of other Capulets and Montagues had appeared and joined the battle. They came rushing out of stores and into the street to defend their fellow servants, their cousins, and their friends. The fighting grew more and more furious as they battled beneath the hot sun. Like a raging fire, the fighting spread in all directions with awesome speed and power.

Just imagine what it would be like watching this scene on a stage. All those actors clanking their swords together, leaping around, charging in all directions, tumbling to the ground—sort of a cross between a ballet and a football game!

Men and women who were shopping stopped to see what was going on. Children playing in the square gazed in wonder. As soon as it became clear that another brawl between the Capulets and Montagues was growing out of control, everyone who didn't belong to one of those families ran for cover.

Shop owners hurried to bring their goods inside, then closed up their shops. For some it was too late. Capulets and Montagues had seized their fruit to launch as missiles at one another. Men crashed into shelves full of fragile pottery. Soon the entire square was crammed with angry fighters thrashing their swords against one another. As the clanging, banging, crashing, and screaming grew louder, it horrified people all over town—except the Capulets and Montagues. All the chaos seemed to make members of those families happy, as though they'd been waiting for a chance to fight.

As he entered the square, old Lord Capulet called to his wife. "Give me my sword, dear!" he shouted. "I'll show those Montagues what's what!"

"You, calling for a sword?" she taunted. "You'd do better to call for a crutch!" But off Lord Capulet went, waving his sword wildly as he staggered toward the battle. His wife hurried after him, trying to drag him back to safety.

The bloody fighting grew so intense it was hard to imagine it would ever stop. But it did stop—suddenly. Two fighters on the edge of town saw something that made them stand still. Others around them looked up too, and stood frozen in place. Swiftly, a stillness swept across the crowd, until all stood, or sat, or lay, gazing up at a sight that sent a chill through their veins. For sitting on his horse, surveying the broken carts, the bloody walls, and the injured bodies was the Prince.

This Prince guy—the ruler of Verona—has everybody in suspense. What in the world is he going to do to them?

"Are you my subjects? Or are you rebels, determined to destroy our entire city?" bellowed the Prince. His voice echoed through the square. "Drop your swords, all of you. Do you hear me? Drop them, I say. Now!"

At once, the hundreds of Capulets and Montagues who'd been drawn into the fight dropped their weapons to the ground. They waited to hear the Prince's words.

"Three times this year, bloody, reckless riots have broken out between your families. Three times Verona has been covered with blood. Shops and homes have been destroyed. Innocent people have been frightened, wounded, and even killed. The hatred between your families is like a constant storm cloud hanging over our city. So the next time I hear about any violence between the Capulets and the Montagues, those responsible will pay with their lives."

With this decree, the Prince tugged the reins of his horse and galloped back up the road toward his castle. Slowly the crowd began to scatter. Friends helped each other up and cared for one another's wounds. Enemies pretended not to notice one another. Some mothers came looking for their sons and were horrified to find them wounded.

2
Broken Heart

One mother came looking for her son, but she couldn't find him anywhere. It was Lady Montague, the wife of Lord Montague himself. Although she couldn't locate her teenage son, Romeo, she did spot his good friend and cousin Benvolio. Do you think Benvolio has any news of Romeo?

"R omeo wasn't in this awful fight, was he, Benvolio?" Lady Montague asked. She was relieved when Benvolio shook his head, but she was still a little concerned. "If he's not with you, or any of his friends, then where is he?" she continued.

"I haven't seen Romeo since dawn, madam," Benvolio replied. "When I was taking an early morning walk, I saw him sitting under a tree watching the sunrise. As I came over to say hello, he hurried away, pretending not to see me. Is everything okay with Romeo?"

"That's what we wanted to ask you," chimed in old Montague, catching up with his wife.

"Every night he sits up by candlelight sighing and sobbing," explained Lady Montague. "Sometimes he goes walking by himself until dawn, and then he locks himself in his room again. He closes all his windows and just sits inside and moans."

"Have you asked him what's wrong?" inquired Benvolio.

"I've asked him," Montague said with a sigh. "His mother's asked him too. But he won't give anyone a hint what the problem is."

Romeo's mother begged, "Do you think you could find out, good Benvolio? Even the smallest clue might help us."

"Look, there is your sad son walking our way now," said Benvolio. "Hurry away so he doesn't suspect we've been talking about him. I'll try to find out what's bothering him."

Montague and his wife followed Benvolio's advice and left. Then Benvolio hurried toward a young man who had a secret that was eating him alive.

"Good day, cousin," said Benvolio as he followed Romeo on a walk that seemed to be leading nowhere.

Finally we get to meet this Romeo we've been hearing so much about!

"It's day?" sighed Romeo.

"Well, the sun *is* shining in the sky, isn't it?" Benvolio pointed out gently.

"It feels like night to me," replied Romeo. "One long, dark, cold night that just drags on and on."

"Do you want to tell me what's making time go so slowly for you?" asked Benvolio.

"Not having the thing that would make time go quickly," was Romeo's strange reply.

As they walked on, Benvolio thought about this last clue his cousin had given him. Suddenly it became clear. "You're in love!" he exclaimed.

"Out," Romeo shot back.

"Out of love?" Benvolio asked.

"Out of favor with the woman I love."

"Aha!" thought Benvolio to himself. "I knew it had something to do with love."

"What's this?" gasped Romeo, when he saw a bench in the square that had been smashed in two. Before Benvolio could explain about the brawl that had just ended, Romeo said, "Never mind, I heard all about it. Our families are swallowed up by hate. And I'm swallowed up by love."

"Can you tell me who you're so mad about?" asked Benvolio.

"Mad is the word, all right!" Romeo answered. "I'm raving like a madman. Without hope. Without light. Without time. Without friends—"

"Wait a minute!" Benvolio broke in. "You're not without friends, Romeo."

"I'm alone, even when I'm with other people," was Romeo's confusing explanation.

"Tell me her name!" insisted Benvolio.

"You want to know whom I love?"

"Yes!"

"Well, if you insist, I'll tell you." Romeo looked to the left, then to the right. Then he whispered in Benvolio's ear. "The truth is, my cousin, I love a woman."

"I guessed that much," answered Benvolio.

"Did you guess her name was Rosaline?" Romeo asked, finally revealing his secret. **Rosaline? Hey, wait a minute. This story's called ROMEO AND JULIET, not ROMEO AND ROSALINE!**

"Rosaline, cousin?" said Benvolio. "She's very beautiful. You certainly do aim high! Have you told Rosaline how you feel?"

"I told her I love her. But she told me she'll never love anyone," confessed Romeo, tears welling up in his eyes.

"Never, ever?" asked Benvolio.

"Never, ever," answered Romeo. "So I'll never, ever be happy."

"Hold on now, Romeo," interrupted Benvolio. "Sure, Rosaline's pretty. But there are lots of beautiful women in Verona. Follow me for the next half hour and I'll point out five women just as beautiful as Rosaline."

Romeo wasn't going to be so easily consoled. "Every other beauty you show me will only make me love my Rosaline more," he insisted. "Rosaline is perfect! Now that I've seen her, I can't settle for less. I need to be alone, cousin. You can't make me forget!"

But Benvolio wasn't about to give up. "You want to bet?" he asked, following close behind his stubborn friend.

Meanwhile, just across the street, two other people were discussing love in a very different way. Their discussion was more formal. More reasonable. More polite. But the person they were talking about would soon come crashing into Romeo's life like a blazing comet.

3
A Party Invitation

So now we meet an Italian named Paris. If you think that's confusing, I once knew a French poodle named Montana.

A young count named Paris searched the crowded streets for Lord Capulet. "Lord Capulet," he called, "have you come to a decision about my question, sir?" Today, as always, Paris's clothes fit perfectly and matched perfectly, and his hair was neatly combed. "Have you decided whether I might have the hand of your fair daughter, Juliet?" **According to the traditions of those days, a father had the authority to choose his daughter's husband.**

Old Lord Capulet shook his head. "I'm afraid the only answer I have for you today is the same answer I had for you yesterday. My child is just a teenager. I hardly think it's time for her to be a wife."

"But my good sir," Paris replied as politely as possible, "there are women younger than Juliet who have made very good mothers."

"Mothers?" gasped Capulet. "Listen, Paris. She's the only child I have. I'm in no hurry for her to get married. But if you do love her, seeing as you're such a gentleman, you're more than welcome to spend time with her. After all, I'm certainly not about to ask Juliet to marry someone she doesn't love. And she doesn't even know you!"

"When may I call on Juliet then, sir?" inquired Paris. "I hope it can be soon."

"It can be tonight, lad!" Capulet answered. "I'm having a big party, and I've invited all my dearest friends and relatives. There will be musicians, and dancing, and feasting. You'll have a chance to get to know my daughter, or any of the other lovely ladies you care to meet. You don't have other plans that will keep you away, I hope?"

"Nothing in this wide world could keep me away, good sir!" replied the eager young count.

"Excellent," said Capulet. "Come here, Peter," he said to one of his servants who was strolling by snacking on a pear.

"Yes, Lord Capulet?" answered the servant, springing to attention as he tossed the pear away behind his back.

"Go through Verona, find the people whose names are written on this guest list, and tell them they're invited to my party tonight!" ordered Capulet.

"But sir—" began Peter, looking worried.

"I've no time to chatter now," Capulet answered. "I've got a million things to do before tonight!"

As Capulet and Paris left, poor Peter found himself in a terrible bind. "Find the people whose names are written on this list?" he whined. "He might as well have asked the shoemaker to sew him a shirt. Or the tailor to make him a nice pair of boots. Or the fisherman to paint his portrait. Or the painter to catch him a big juicy catfish. How could he ask me to do this job when I can't read a word? I'd better find somebody smart to help me out, or nobody will show up at the party!" **During this period, very few servants like Peter went to school or learned how to read or write.**

Just then, Romeo and Benvolio came wandering by. Peter could tell they were well-educated because of the complex debate they were having.

"Well, at the very least, Romeo, you must admit that a new pain can make you forget about an old one," reasoned Benvolio.

"You want to show me other women to add to my pain?" asked Romeo.

"Maybe the new pain could be relieved, if the woman who causes it isn't as cold-hearted as Rosaline."

"If only one disease could cure me of another," Romeo said. "But there's nothing that can rescue me from the horrible, terrible..." Romeo's speech trailed off as he noticed Peter standing there staring at him and Benvolio. "Can I help you?" Romeo asked.

"Excuse me, sirs," said Peter, "but can you read?"

"I can," answered Romeo.

"Really?" Peter perked up. "You mean you can read anything you see?"

"I can read words, sentences, even whole paragraphs!" responded Romeo.

Delighted, Peter handed the note to Romeo. "It's a list, isn't it?" Romeo said as he looked at it. "And it's a long one! It says 'Count Martino and his wife and daughters, Count Anselm and his beautiful sisters, the Lady Widow Vitruvio, my nephew Tybalt...'"

Romeo read down the list slowly, until he got to a name that made his heart race: "'My fair niece Rosaline'! Why are all the names of all these people on this list?" Romeo asked the servant.

"They're all coming to the house!" replied Peter.

"To what house?" Romeo demanded.

"To my master's house."

"Please tell me the name of your master," Romeo pleaded.

"My master is the great Lord Capulet, and the guests are all coming to his house tonight. As long as you're not a Montague, you're welcome to come too. Thanks for your help, gentlemen!"

As Peter left, Benvolio sensed that his lovesick friend was excited. "You're not planning to buy a mask and drop by on a certain party tonight, Romeo?"

"You've read my mind, friend."

"Pick up two masks. I'll come along," offered Benvolio.

"To watch me suffer?"

"No, to make sure you spend a little time noticing someone besides Rosaline. I'll point out other pretty faces, other sweet smiles, other lovely eyes. I'll prove to you that there are others just as beautiful as Rosaline—and a lot more friendly."

The idea that he'd be able to notice any other woman besides Rosaline seemed so ridiculous to Romeo that he did something he hadn't done in days: he laughed aloud.

> **Do Montagues intend to crash**
> **The Capulets' big family bash?**
> **A risk so great they're taking now!**
> **Alas! Alack! Forsooth! Bow wow!**

Okay—so I'm not Shakespeare.
But he wasn't a cute little dog.

4
A Mother's Proposal

Now we meet the play's main women characters: Lady Capulet, the Nurse, and of course, Juliet. Believe it or not, in Shakespeare's day, Lady Capulet and the Nurse were played by men, and Juliet was played by a boy! At that time, it was considered improper for females to perform on stage in plays. Of course, nowadays, anyone can perform in Shakespeare's plays. Some of us are still waiting for the "all dog" version of ROMEO AND JULIET.

"*N*urse! Where is my daughter? Tell her I wish to speak with her!" Lady Capulet called out from her bedroom in the enormous Capulet house, as a servant brushed out her hair.

"I did tell her you were looking for her," replied the Nurse, a stout woman of about fifty, as she came trotting into the room. "*Juliet!*" she shouted. "Where are you? Your mother wants you!"

"Here I am!" said Juliet as she came in.

Lady Capulet excused the servant who had been brushing her hair. The Nurse was allowed to stay, since she was Juliet's special guardian. She had cared for Juliet since she was a baby.

ROMEO AND JULIET is considered a tragedy because some very sad things happen. But every once in a while, funny characters like the Nurse show up to give the audience a few laughs. These laughs in the middle of a tragedy are called comic relief.

"I have a very serious subject to discuss with you, young lady," Lady Capulet began, "so I'd like your undivided attention."

"Yes, Mother," replied Juliet.

"You are growing up so quickly—" Lady Capulet began.

"Indeed!" interrupted the Nurse. "In two weeks she will be fourteen. I know that because the great earthquake was eleven years ago, and Juliet was only three then. So if she was three years old eleven years ago, then she would be fourteen now."

"Yes, I know that," Lady Capulet snapped. She often had to put up with the Nurse's interruptions. "As I was saying—"

"I remember Juliet so well at that age," the Nurse babbled on. "She was always running about. One day she fell and cut her forehead. I recall my husband— God rest his soul—picked her up. 'Did you fall down?' he asked her. Then—"

"Enough, Nurse," said Lady Capulet, trying to continue.

"I know I've said enough," confessed the Nurse. "Far more than enough. It's just that you were such a darling child, Juliet. When I remember—"

"You'd better stop talking, Nurse," whispered Juliet. She could see her mother was growing angry.

"I'll stop, I'll stop," promised the Nurse. "But I do swear, Juliet, you were the cutest baby. I'll die happy if I can live to see you married."

"That's just the subject I wanted to talk about!" exclaimed Lady Capulet, finally getting the Nurse's attention. "Juliet, have you thought much about getting married?"

"Married?" asked Juliet. Her mother might as well have asked if she'd thought much about dressing as a boy and joining a troupe of traveling players. "Well, Mother, it's an honor I haven't even considered."

"It is an honor, indeed," the Nurse chimed in. "To be married is a great honor. If you can catch the right man, of course."

"You might give it some thought," continued Lady Capulet. "Because the count Paris wants you to be his bride."

"Paris?" exclaimed the Nurse. "Why, he's the perfect man! He's handsome. He's rich. He's loved by everybody in town. He's a count. And what a terrific dresser!"

"He is very well thought of," added Juliet's mother.

"*Very* well thought of," echoed the Nurse. "One of the most respected people in all of Verona. In fact, if there's anyone more popular than Paris, I can't think of him!"

"So what do you say, Juliet?" asked her mother. "Could you love him?"

Juliet shrugged her shoulders.

"Tonight you'll see him at our feast," the Lady continued. "If he approaches you, speak with him. Examine his character."

"And look him over too, Juliet!" the Nurse added. "Sorry, my lady, but Paris is one of the most handsome men in Verona!"

"If you'd like me to speak with Paris tonight, Mother, I will," answered Juliet.

Juliet and the Nurse began to go through Juliet's enormous wardrobe to pick out just the right dress for Juliet to wear to the party.

Paris too was planning what he'd wear that evening. He dropped by the tailor to try on a new shirt he'd ordered just for the occasion, one with especially puffy sleeves.

Meanwhile, a group of young men who weren't expected at the party were busy deciding what they would wear too. But unlike the others, they were planning to go in disguise.

Hold on. Juliet's going to be meeting Paris? And Romeo's coming to see Rosaline? At this point I'd have to call the play ROMEO AND ROSALINE or PARIS AND JULIET!

5
Mercutio's Joke

So! Our merry Montagues intend to crash the Capulet party by wearing masks! How bold! How daring! How fashionable? In the days in which our story takes place, it wasn't uncommon for young men to come to a party wearing masks. Sometimes they wore the masks as part of a little show they'd offer to do at the party. Sometimes they just wore the masks for fun.

No one in the streets of Verona that night was puzzled by the sight of a dozen young men wearing masks as they made their way through town. Romeo, Benvolio, and a group of their Montague friends jumped at the chance to get into a party, regardless of who was hosting it. As they hurried along, the anxious teens all sang loudly, joked, danced around, punched one another, and laughed—all except Romeo, of course.

"We're going to make you dance tonight," Benvolio insisted.

"Not me," claimed Romeo. "You with your merry

hearts can dance. I have a soul of lead that weighs me down to the ground."

"Nonsense, lover-boy!" shouted Mercutio, the group's wildest member. He was always fun to have around for his crazy stunts and gags, although he could be tiresome after a while. "You *will* dance tonight, Romeo. So borrow Cupid's wings, and fly! Fly!"

"I'm too wounded by Cupid's arrow to fly with his wings," Romeo replied.

"If love hurts you, hurt love back!" Mercutio retorted. "Give little baby Cupid a good swift kick!" **Cupid is a mythical god of love. Any person Cupid shoots with his magical bow and arrow instantly falls in love. I don't know about Mercutio, but I personally wouldn't give a swift kick to anybody with a magical bow and arrow.**

Everybody laughed at Mercutio's clever answer—everyone except Romeo. "I have a feeling something tragic is going to happen tonight," he said.

Mercutio was getting pretty sick of Romeo's moping. "And what, may I ask, gives you that idea?"

"A dream I had," Romeo replied.

For Mercutio, this was the last straw. He couldn't stand the way some guys who fell in love got all romantic, started writing poetry, and thought their dreams were full of important meaning. So Mercutio launched into one of his bitter, mocking speeches.

At this point in the play, Mercutio goes into a long speech, called a monologue. When a Shakespearean actor gets to do a monologue, it's like when a guitarist plays a solo. Mercutio really gets to have fun with this monologue. He uses his imagination to create a character named Queen Mab to tease Romeo.

"A dream you had?" he began. "So you had a little dream? Well then, Queen Mab has been with you, Romeo! She's a nasty fairy, the size of a pebble. She creeps into judges' noses at night while they're asleep and pulls out their nose hairs. Then she lands on bankers' fingers and makes them dream about money. Then she darts through certain teenagers' brains and makes them dream about lovey-dovey, scrumptious-dumptious *love*. Then she lands on these lovers' lips to test their breath. If it stinks, she gives them blisters on their chins and warts on their toes. Then she twists the sweaty hair on their necks into knots, and she pinches and spits and tears and—"

"Calm down, Mercutio," said Romeo, putting his arm around his friend. "You're talking about nothing."

"Exactly," proclaimed Mercutio, catching his breath. "I'm talking about dreams, which mean absolutely nothing. So stop thinking about your depressing dreams and think about laughing."

Not wishing to make Mercutio angry again, Romeo kept his worries to himself as they all walked down the street. Soon they arrived at the splendid Capulet house. They made sure their masks were in place and knocked on the door. When the door opened, what sights the young men beheld! A dozen musicians were playing stringed instruments, pipes, and drums of all kinds, and hundreds of people from all over town were dancing. Servants carried enormous trays of snacks. The long tables lining the walls were decked with luscious cakes, fruits, salads, and meats.

Within moments the masked Montague men were dancing, feasting, singing, and laughing. They fit in perfectly!

But one young Montague stood still, not moving, not speaking, just staring at a sight that left him paralyzed.

Who is this young Montague who cannot move or speak? And what does he see? Can you feel the suspense?

6
Love at First Sight

"Welcome!" shouted jolly Lord Capulet. He called to a servant, "Quick, you! Bring some cakes for these young men in the masks. Welcome to the grand Capulet feast, gentlemen."

Capulet was the kind of host who wanted everyone to be happy at all costs. It was great to be a guest at one of his parties. Being a servant at his parties was a different story.

"Bring more light here!" he shouted at his servants. "We need more light, I say! Bring more torches. People are bumping into each other. Leave those torches here at once. Now it's too hot. Too hot, I'm telling you. The dancers are sweating! What are all those torches doing here? Take them away. Away, I said! Are you deaf? And play louder, musicians! For what I'm paying, you can play louder than that!"

At one point Lord Capulet took a brief break from shouting at his servants to chat with an old friend. "Remember when we used to wear masks and go to parties like this, cousin?" he asked.

"That hasn't been for thirty years," his cousin replied.

"What wild kids we were," Capulet remembered

fondly. "Thirty years? It can't be. Really! My, my, how the time has flown. More light over here! Bring some torches!"

Lord Capulet's greatest pleasure was to see everyone dancing. As long as everybody danced, he considered the party a complete success, so he did his best to get everyone onto the floor.

"Come on, you ladies," he shouted across the room. "You can chit-chat any time. Any woman who refuses to dance must have corns on her feet. Is that it? Have you got big, painful corns on your toes? Well then, why aren't you dancing? Dance, dance!"

Just about everybody *was* dancing. The floor was packed with bodies leaping and spinning about in time to the music. But one young man wasn't dancing. He stood off to the side in the shadows, staring at a young lady he'd never seen before as she laughed and danced in a circle with her friends. The young man was Romeo. And the woman he watched was not Rosaline, but Juliet, Lord Capulet's daughter.

"Her face has a brighter glow than the torches!" Romeo said to himself, lifting his mask to get a better look. "She's like a gorgeous jewel, lighting up the room all by herself. Her beauty is too great for the world. She's so beautiful it hurts to look at her. But it feels wonderful too. I could stand here and look at her until the end of time."

In the play, Shakespeare has Romeo say:

**"Did my heart love till now? forswear it, sight!
For I ne'er saw true beauty till this night."**

**In other words, one look at Juliet and he's totally
forgotten about Rosaline!**

When the music stopped, Romeo got an idea.
"She's standing by herself all of a sudden," he
thought. "Now's my chance to speak to her. I'm
scared to death, but love is making me brave. Here I
go!"

So Romeo made his way across the crowded floor
toward his new love, not noticing anything or anyone
else. But someone noticed him. Tybalt, the Capulet
who was most anxious to fight, recognized Romeo,
whose mask was still raised up to his forehead.

"Boy!" Tybalt barked at his servant. "Go and get
me my sword this instant!"

**Uh-oh! Tybalt loves a fight. Will he
challenge Romeo before Romeo gets to
speak with Juliet? Will the Capulets and
the Montagues continue their fighting
ways despite the warning of the
Prince? Read on!**

7
First Meeting

Lord Capulet overheard Tybalt calling for his sword. "What's wrong, Tybalt?" Capulet asked his angry nephew. "Not having a good time? Why don't you dance, or have some more food?"

"I've just seen one of our enemies, Uncle," was Tybalt's bitter reply. "A snake from the house of Montague has come to make fun of our party. Anyone who breaks into our house deserves to be slaughtered—and I'll be glad to do the job."

"What are you talking about?" asked Capulet. "A Montague? Where?"

"There, Uncle," said Tybalt, pointing across the room with the sword that had just been handed to him. "Slithering across our floor is Romeo, the snake who has invaded our feast."

"Yes, it does look like Romeo," agreed Capulet. "But leave him alone. He's not causing any trouble. To tell you the truth, people say that he's quite a nice fellow. So just ignore him, all right? If you respect my wishes, you'll put away your sword and wipe that angry scowl from your face."

"I have a right to be angry when a snake is in our house," Tybalt retorted. "I won't allow him to stay."

"*You* won't allow him?" yelled Capulet, losing his

temper. "*You* won't allow him? So it's your party, is it? And your house? You're not the master here. You *will* put up with him, young man. Do you understand? I won't let you turn my party into a bloody brawl."

"It's humiliating, Uncle," Tybalt whined.

"Humiliating, is it?" railed Capulet. "You spoiled little brat. I've told you to put away that sword. I'm not going to tell you again. Put it away!"

Tybalt's uncle was shouting so loud that people were starting to stare. Reluctantly, Tybalt did as Capulet asked. "I'll put away the sword for now," he said to himself.

What a hothead! Tybalt hates Romeo, but Romeo is only thinking about his true love. (That would be Juliet, in case you just joined us.)

Meanwhile, Romeo's heart was beating like mad. He had crept up behind Juliet, and was now within inches of her. Suddenly he stopped and just stood there, with no idea what to say, or what to do. He held his breath, frozen for what seemed like ten years. Then, without thinking, he suddenly grabbed her hand.

Juliet gasped. She didn't know who this strange boy was, but as she looked into his eyes, she felt as though she could trust him completely. It felt like they'd been best friends all their lives.

"I'm sorry for taking your hand," Romeo said. "I know I have no right to. Your hand is so beautiful and

45

delicate it's like a beautiful palace. My poor hands are like beggars tramping through a palace in dirty boots. May I make up for the harm my hands have done to your hand with a kiss?"

Romeo wasn't thinking about what he was saying. The words were just pouring out. But to Juliet they were poetry.

"You shouldn't insult such sweet hands as yours," Juliet replied. "Your hands are so wonderful they should be doing wonderful things. Like praying."

Juliet gently removed her hand from Romeo's grasp, turned to face him, and held both her hands in front of her face with the fingers spread wide apart.

Romeo took her cue, and raised his hands too. They placed their ten fingertips together, like two pairs of praying hands.

"Of course," continued Romeo, his heart pounding as if it were about to burst out of his chest, "when people pray, they don't just use their hands. They also use their lips."

"That's right," agreed Juliet. "You can't whisper a prayer without using your lips."

"Well then," said Romeo, "let our lips do what our hands do, and come together to pray."

"Let the praying begin," Juliet said. And no sooner had she said it, than Romeo moved his head slowly toward hers and gave her a single, gentle kiss.

"Juliet!" called the Nurse. "Your mother wants to talk to you!"

As Juliet hurried toward her mother, Romeo asked the name of his new love. "Juliet's her name, lad," replied the Nurse. "And her mother's the lady of the house."

"A Capulet!" he gasped. "My family's enemy owns my heart."

"Come on, Romeo," urged Benvolio. "The party's dying down. Let's head into town. Are you coming?"

As his friends dragged Romeo away, Capulet showed his guests to the door. "Leaving already, people? Yes, it is getting late. Well, thank you for coming. What a night! Delightful and splendid, wasn't it? Servant, give them more light over here or they'll bump into a tree!"

"Who's that going through the door, Nurse?" asked Juliet.

"I don't know," confessed the Nurse.

"Well, ask his name, Nurse! Please?" begged Juliet.

Juliet paced back and forth as she waited for her answer. "Please don't let him be married!" she thought.

"His name is Romeo," the Nurse revealed. "He's a Montague—the only son of our mortal enemy."

Juliet was crushed. "My only love, a member of the only family I hate!" she gasped.

"Come on, Juliet, it's time for bed," said the Nurse.

Juliet headed up the stairs to her room, where she would force herself to go to sleep. Or so she thought....

Romeo and Juliet fall head over heels in love one minute, only to find out that their families are lifelong enemies the next!

8
Jumping the Wall

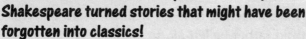

Isn't this an exciting story? You might be surprised to learn that this story didn't come only from Shakespeare's imagination. He based his plays on poems, myths, fables, historical events, and other plays. Shakespeare turned stories that might have been forgotten into classics!

As the Montague men made their way from the Capulet house, they passed through a wide garden surrounded by a stone wall. Benvolio, Mercutio, and the others boasted to one another about all the girls they'd danced with at the party. But Romeo didn't hear a word they said. He was lost in a dream.

As the young men passed through the gate leading out to the road, a gatekeeper wished them good night and shut the gate behind them. When the gate slammed shut, Romeo gazed longingly back at the house. In a flash, he came up with a plan.

Slipping away from his friends, Romeo dashed away and hid behind a bush. "Can I go forward when my heart is here with Juliet?" he thought. As he heard his friends coming closer, he scurried behind another bush. Then he leaped right over the wall to the Capulets' garden. Holding his breath, he listened a moment as his friends approached. They had just noticed he was gone.

"Romeo? Cousin Romeo?" called Benvolio.

"Why are you calling him by his old name, Benvolio?" asked Mercutio. "Lover-boy! Madman! Poet! Oh, miserable victim of Cupid, can you hear us?"

"I have a feeling he does hear us," said Benvolio, "but would rather be left alone."

"Should we leave you alone, Mister Dream-head?" taunted Mercutio. "Should we let you go moping in your marvelous madness, O Prince of Poetry, King of Kissing, O Leader of Lovesick Longing?"

Actors playing Mercutio really enjoy delivering the many funny lines Shakespeare wrote for the character. Though Romeo is the biggest, most important male role in the play, many actors would rather play the witty Mercutio.

Benvolio told Mercutio to hurry, but Mercutio hadn't finished making fun of their lovesick friend. "Now he'll lie out under the stars writing poems, and he'll be writing out there until dawn. And so I bid you adieu, poor poet. Poor sick madman. Poor lunatic!"

By now, the group had dragged Mercutio far enough away that Romeo could barely hear him. "It's easy for him to make fun of people in love, because he's never been in love himself," Romeo thought. "If he had, he'd understand."

As the noise of his friends' voices died away, Romeo began to roam around the Capulet grounds, which was a very dangerous thing for him to do—if he was caught by his family's enemies, he would be killed. He heard something stir on the other side of a towering oak and froze. Then he realized that it was only an owl perched in a branch over his head.

As he crept past a row of trees that led along the side of the house, Romeo heard soft voices and saw two guards seated on a bench outside the stable door. He dashed back toward the front and slid behind a row of bushes lining the wall. The bushes went all the way around to the other side of the house.

Romeo held his breath for as long as he could, afraid that someone would hear him. Finally he reached the corner and slid around it. There he found another row of bushes, lower than the row that lined the wall in back. Now Romeo had to bend his knees as he inched along so his cap wouldn't poke out over the top of the hedge.

When the row of bushes ended, Romeo leaned out and peered into the yard. It was completely dark, except for the light of the full moon. There were no doors on this side of the house, nor were there any guards. There also wasn't any place to hide, except for one tall, leafy tree that stood next to the house and reached up toward a balcony.

"I could make a dash to that tree," Romeo thought. "Those guards are pretty far away from here. They looked lazy, sitting there mumbling to one another. As long as they don't go for a midnight stroll, they won't hear my footsteps. They won't hear me climbing up the tree either. I could climb high into the branches and leap onto the balcony and into the house of my love!"

If he'd stopped to think, Romeo would have realized his plan had problems. For example, once he got inside the house, how would he find Juliet? There were hundreds of rooms in the Capulet mansion. But Romeo wasn't planning that far ahead just yet. He was following his heart. He was determined, desperate, and a little bit insane with love.

There wasn't much that could stop Romeo from making his way toward the house. Then, suddenly, something did. As he dashed toward the tree beneath the balcony, light came pouring out. Someone had lit a candle in the room inside, casting light out through the balcony over Romeo's head.

"How did they hear me?" he said to himself in panic. "I was creeping so quietly that I could hardly hear my footsteps myself! What awful luck! Now they're going to send the guards down to catch me and beat me because I'm a Montague. Then they'll have me arrested for being on their property. I'll be sent away to prison and I won't get to see Juliet's face ever again!"

But Romeo's luck wasn't awful at all. In fact, just the opposite was true. For after an instant of panic, Romeo realized that the candle hadn't been lit by an angry parent or a suspicious watchman. It had been lit by Juliet. She stepped out onto the balcony and began to speak.

Balcony? She's on a balcony? When you've got Romeo looking up at Juliet, who's standing on a balcony, you've got— Could it really be? Yes, I think it must be the most romantic scene of all time: the balcony scene.

9
The Balcony

In the play this is where Romeo says:

"But, soft! what light through yonder window breaks?
It is the east, and Juliet is the sun!"

I love that verse!

Romeo was so dazed by his good luck that he could hardly stand up. He held on to the trunk of the tree for support and stared up at the face he adored.

"What a dazzling light pours from that balcony," he thought. "What a gorgeous glow...and it all comes from her face! Here it is, the middle of the night, and I could swear I'm watching a sunrise. My Juliet is the beautiful sun that warms the whole world."

After staring out across the moonlit yard, Juliet began to move her lips as though she were speaking. But she didn't make a sound.

"Who is she speaking to?" wondered Romeo. "I wish she were speaking to me. But no, she's speaking to someone far more worthy than me. Look, Juliet's eyes glow more brightly than any star! Those eyes pour brightness down across her delicate cheek and light up the night."

Without warning, Juliet did make a sound. It was a small sound: a single sigh.

"She speaks!" Romeo thought. "Oh, please speak again. For your voice is heavenly music, like angels singing in harmony as they float through the clouds."

Juliet had no idea anyone was listening to her every word. "Oh Romeo, Romeo," she sighed. "Why do you have to have that name—Montague? I wish you'd just leave your father and change your name. Or if you won't, swear that you love me, and I'll stop being a Capulet forever."

Hey, that sounds familiar. This is the part in the play when Juliet says:

**"Romeo, Romeo, wherefore art thou Romeo?
  Deny thy father and refuse thy name."**

**Wherefore doesn't mean where, it means why.
So she's saying "Why are you Romeo, a Montague,
the enemy of my family?" Wherefore can't
I come up with incredible lines like
that?**

Romeo was dumbstruck. "She's thinking about me, just like I've been thinking about her!" He wanted to answer her but longed to hear more of the voice that was music to his ears.

"It's your name that's my enemy," Juliet continued. "You'd be you, even if you weren't a Montague. What is *Montague* anyway? It's not your hand, or your foot, or your arm, or your face, or any other part of your body. Oh, why couldn't you have some other last name?"

As Juliet continued, she leaned forward over the balcony to pluck a leaf off the branch of the nearby tree. She leaned so far over that Romeo was sure she would see him. But still she didn't know he was there.

"What's all this fuss about names anyway?" she wondered. "If we called roses dandelions, they'd smell just as sweet. And Romeo would be just as wonderful if he were called Othello or Prospero. Oh Romeo, get rid of your name, which isn't any part of you. In exchange for your name, take all of me!"

In the play, this is where Juliet says:

**"What's in a name? that which we call a rose
By any other word would smell as sweet."**

It's true too! Try the test yourself.

"I will!" shouted Romeo, no longer able to listen in silence. "Tell me you love me and I'll be born all over again with a completely different name!"

Startled, Juliet sprang back from the balcony. "Who's hiding out there in our yard spying on me?" she called down into the darkness.

"I have no idea how to tell you who I am since I hate my name!" Romeo answered. "My name is your enemy, so I refuse to use it. If it were written down, I'd tear it up into a hundred pieces!"

At once Juliet recognized the voice that called to her. She smiled and leaned over the balcony's railing. "You're Romeo, aren't you?" she asked. "And you're a Montague."

"I'm neither of those," Romeo answered, "if you don't want me to be."

"How in the world did you get here?" she asked Romeo. "The walls around our house are very tall and hard to climb. Aren't you worried about the watchmen? And my father? Do you have any idea what they'd do if they found you out here?"

"My love for you gave me wings, so I flew right over the walls," Romeo replied. "Did you think a heap of stones could keep out true love? Let your relatives do what they like to me. Any pain they could cause would be wiped out by the joy of this moment."

"If they find you, they'll kill you!" Juliet warned.

"Your beauty gives me strength," Romeo explained. "Inspired by your eyes, I could beat an army single-handedly!"

"Seriously, Romeo," she persisted. "They must not find you."

"Let them find me!" Romeo exclaimed.

"How did you know which window was mine?" she asked.

"Love showed me the way," he answered. "I'd be able to find my way to you even if you were hidden on the other side of the world."

"I would never have said all those things if I had known you were there," Juliet confessed, suddenly embarrassed. She paused and thought for a moment. Then she asked, "Do you love me?"

Before Romeo could answer, Juliet continued. "I know you'll say yes, and that you'll swear you love me. But people swear they'll love each other forever all the time. And their love doesn't last a week! If you really do love me, say it and really mean it."

Ready to prove his love with a kiss, Romeo shimmied up the tree, climbed into the branches, and was perched on a long limb, from which he could reach Juliet's outstretched hands. Once again Romeo tried to swear his love. "My dear Juliet, I swear by that moon, that as long as the seas rush across the—"

"Don't swear by the moon!" Juliet interrupted. "The moon's always changing. Every night it's a little different. And sometimes it disappears altogether. I don't want your love to change every day. Or to disappear, ever!"

"So what should I swear by?" asked Romeo, at a loss for words.

"Don't swear at all," was Juliet's answer. "Or if

you will, just swear by yourself, since you're the man of my dreams."

"If you'd like," Romeo began, not really knowing how to swear by himself. "Uh, in the name of—"

"No, don't swear at all," she cut him off again. "All your promises are making me nervous. This is happening so quickly."

Romeo didn't want Juliet to feel rushed, but he didn't want to leave her either. So, as kind as her next words were, they disappointed him. "Good night, my sweet," she sighed. Romeo gripped her hand even more tightly. "Let's let our love grow slowly," she explained, "like a flower that spreads its petals a little bit more every day. I hope your sleep is as sweet as the joy I'm feeling right now in my heart."

"Will you make me go without your promise?" asked Romeo.

"My promise of what?"

"Your promise that you love me," he answered gently.

"I gladly give you my promise that I love you with all my heart," she responded. "Yet all of a sudden I wish I could take back that promise."

"Take it back?" he asked, alarmed. "Why would you want to take back your promise that you love me?"

Helllooo! Start flipping the book pages and check out the action . . . . Woo-cha!

"So I could give it to you all over again, and again, and again," she replied. "My love is as enormous as the sea. No matter how much of it I could give you, there's always more."

In the play, Juliet says:

"My bounty is as boundless as the sea,
My love as deep; the more I give to thee,
the more I have, for both are infinite."

Juliet glanced back into her room. She heard the Nurse calling to her from down the hall. "Coming, Nurse!" Juliet said. She gestured to Romeo that she'd be back, then hurried into her room.

Romeo was thrilled beyond belief. He swung on the branch like a monkey, then let go and dropped to the ground in a single leap. He lay on his back, giggling quietly, staring up at the stars.

"How do I know I'm not dreaming?" he thought. "This could all be a dream. It's way too quick, too strange, too perfect to be real. Oh well, if it *is* a dream, I hope I never wake up!"

As Juliet hurried back out to her balcony, she called down to her giddy friend in a whisper. "I only have time for two more words, Romeo: Good night!"

But in fact Juliet had more than two words to say. She followed her good night with an offer that left Romeo shocked—and thrilled. "If your love really is serious," she whispered breathlessly, "and you'd like to marry me, and you can find someone willing to marry us, let me know, and I'll be yours for as long as I live."

Romeo could hardly believe his ears. He wanted to shout "Yes!" at the top of his lungs, but he was too astounded to speak. As the Nurse called to Juliet again, Juliet wished Romeo "a thousand good nights" and dashed inside.

"A thousand good nights from sweet Juliet would kill me," he said softly to the stars. "Having to say good night to her just once is unbearable!"

Once again Juliet appeared at the window and called softly to Romeo. "So when will I hear from you about the marriage plans?" she asked.

"I know just the man to do the job," was Romeo's swift answer. "Give me a little time to work out the details—a day at the most."

"By this time tomorrow, then," she said.

"It will seem like twenty years until then," Romeo added.

"Like a million years," said Juliet. She had no idea how he'd work out the details, or how he'd let her know what they were. She just trusted that Romeo would find a way. For a moment they just stood there gazing at each other, with no idea what to say. "I had something to say, but I forget what it was," Juliet confessed.

Romeo was happy to wait while she tried to remember what she was going to say. And Juliet was glad to keep forgetting what she meant to say, just so she could keep him in her company. Romeo didn't mind. He would easily have made that small spot of grass on which he was standing his home, as long as he could keep gazing up at her face.

"It will be morning soon," Juliet said at last, breaking the silence. "I guess you should go. But I wish I could keep you from going far. I wish you were a little bird tied to my finger by a string. Then you could fly a bit, but you'd always have to come right back into my palm."

"If I were your bird, you wouldn't need a string," answered Romeo. "Perching on your hand and staring at your face would be the perfect spot for me."

They ran out of things to say again, and stood there silently gazing at one another for a minute or two more.

"Good night," Juliet finally said.

"Good night," Romeo echoed.

Neither budged.

"Good night," Juliet said again.

"Good night," Romeo said again.

There was a silence.

"Saying good night to you is so sad I could keep on saying good night until tomorrow," Juliet confessed.

At this point in the play Juliet says:

**"Good night, good night: parting is such sweet sorrow,
That I shall say good night till it be morrow."**

Do you love that poetry as much as I do?

As she blew him a kiss, Romeo turned to wander away. Then he charged to the tree once more, yanked himself up to her window, and gently touched her face. They kissed again, until the Nurse called Juliet away. Romeo did finally depart—though not to go to bed.

By now it's so late that the night's almost over. And Romeo's still not going to bed? Where else in the world could he be going?

10
A Visit to the Friar

So now we're meeting Romeo's friend Friar Laurence. A friar is like a priest that people would go to when they had problems.

As the first pink rays of dawn chased away the darkness of night, Friar Laurence rose, dressed his portly frame in his brown hooded robe, and began attending to his duties in the church. Though his main duty was listening to confessions, it was too early for anyone to be visiting. At this early hour, a friar would normally light the candles in the church, polish holy relics, or study the Bible.

But Friar Laurence had a special hobby that he liked to pursue at the crack of dawn each day: collecting plants. This morning, like most others, the aging Friar went into the garden behind the church with his basket to see how his plants were doing.

He was always delighted when a beautiful flower was ready to be plucked. But he didn't just care for plants that were pretty to look at. Weird plants, rare plants, prickly plants, sticky plants, smelly plants, and even poisonous weeds were of great interest to the

Friar. He wasn't interested in plants for their looks, but for their uses. He believed that everything on earth had been put there for a reason, so he felt every plant could be of great use to people. For this reason, he carefully examined each unique plant he could find. He crushed, dissolved, and blended his plants together to make medicines and potions of all kinds.

This morning, crouched on all fours, he came upon a tiny purple flower. "Within the tiny leaf of this weak little flower are two very different, very powerful forces," Friar Laurence marveled, a look of wonder crossing his kind, gentle face. "If you smell the flower, its sweet aroma fills you with joy. But if you taste even the smallest piece, this little flower can leave you completely paralyzed, appearing to be dead." He plucked the small purple flower and dropped it into his basket.

"Good morning, Father!" the Friar heard a young man's voice call.

"Bless you, whoever is up so early," he replied. As Romeo approached, the Friar became concerned. "My son, if you're up this early, you must be very upset about something. It has to do with Rosaline again, I'm sure."

"Oh, no, Father," Romeo exclaimed. "I've forgotten about Rosaline completely."

The Friar was relieved by this news, for Romeo had been complaining to him every day of the grief

Rosaline caused him. But the Friar was still curious about why Romeo had come so early.

In a flood of words, Romeo attempted to explain. "I've been at a party with the enemy of my family."

"I can't help you if I don't understand what you're talking about," said the Friar. "Now tell me again, but this time simply and slowly."

Romeo caught his breath and explained to the Friar that he had fallen in love with Juliet of the house of Capulet, and that she had fallen in love with him too. "The only thing we need now," Romeo added, "is for you to marry us today."

"What?" the Friar yelped. Romeo's extreme behavior had surprised him before, but this sudden change left the Friar baffled. "Is Rosaline, whom you loved so much, so soon forgotten?"

Romeo tried to explain, but the Friar was only beginning his lesson. "How silly your heart is, that you fall deeply in love with a different woman every minute!"

"But Father—" Romeo tried to break in, but the Friar wasn't through.

"Look! Here's the stain of a tear for Rosaline that hasn't dried yet. Maybe that's because you left it there only yesterday! And now Rosaline's erased from your memory? Young man, you leave me speechless."

"You told me to put aside my love for Rosaline, remember?" Romeo asked.

"I didn't mean you should get rid of one love to make room for another," answered the Friar.

"This love is completely different," Romeo insisted.

"How?" the Friar demanded.

"Well, for one thing," Romeo replied, "the lady I love now loves me back with a love that will last forever."

The Friar wondered—could the love of these two young people bring the feuding families together? Finally the Friar spoke. "I will help you, for I think the love between you and Juliet may end the terrible hatred between the Montagues and the Capulets. Now here is what we will do...."

What plan does the good Friar have up his sleeve? Can this plan resolve years of family hatred? We'll soon find out!

11
A Secret Marriage

Juliet knew she could trust the Nurse, so she sent the Nurse into town to find out Romeo's plan for their marriage. Juliet can hardly wait for the Nurse to come back and tell her what is going to happen. The scene between Juliet and the Nurse is one of the funniest in the whole play.

Juliet could hardly sit still as she waited for her Nurse to return with word from Romeo. "I sent her out at nine o'clock, and now it's nearly noon!" she fretted. "Love's messenger should not take so long! If only Romeo and I could send our thoughts to each other! Then each of us would know right away what the other was thinking."

Just then the Nurse hobbled into the room. Juliet jumped up to greet her. "My dear Nurse, what news do you bring?"

"Oh, I am so tired," the Nurse complained, sitting down heavily in a chair. "I'm not used to all this running around. My bones ache!"

"But what did Romeo say?" Juliet asked impatiently.

"Wait a minute, child. Can't you see I am out of breath?"

"How can you be out of breath when you have the breath to tell me that?" Juliet cried. "Your excuses take longer to tell than news from Romeo ever could!"

"Oh, yes, Romeo," the Nurse said. "He is a fine-looking boy, for sure, and he seems like a nice enough fellow. By the way, have you had your dinner yet?"

"My dinner? Who cares about that?" Juliet said. She was ready to tear her hair out with impatience.

"Oh, my head aches," the Nurse moaned. "And my back too." Juliet hurried to rub the older woman's back. "No, not there, my dear. On the other side. I tell you, I am too old for all this running about."

"Sweet Nurse, I am very sorry you don't feel well," Juliet said, trying hard to be polite. "But please, tell my what my true love said."

"Your true love says, like an honest gentleman, and a courteous and kind and handsome one... Where is your mother?"

"Where is my mother?" Juliet shrieked. "What sort of answer is that? 'Your true love says, like an honest gentleman, where is your mother?'"

"Don't be rude to me, or you can deliver your messages yourself," the Nurse said sulkily.

"Oh, Nurse, please!" Juliet begged.

"All right, all right," the Nurse grumbled. "You must go to Friar Laurence's church today. There you will find the man who will make you his wife."

Juliet blushed with pleasure and covered her cheeks with her hands. Her Nurse laughed to see the girl so happy. "Hurry," the older woman said. "Romeo is waiting for you."

Indeed, Romeo was already waiting at Friar Laurence's church, and he was just as impatient to see Juliet as she was to see him. But the Friar was growing nervous. "Oh heavens, please smile upon this holy act," he prayed. "Don't punish us later with sorrow."

"Amen, amen!" said Romeo. "But I'm not worried about sorrow anymore. Nothing can ruin the joy I feel when I am near Juliet. One minute with her fills me with enough happiness to cancel out a lifetime of pain!"

Romeo's confidence only made the Friar more nervous. These people he was about to marry were so young. Did they have any idea what they were getting into? They were playing with fire, taking a very dangerous risk.

"Once we're married, even death won't frighten me," Romeo said. "It will be enough for me just to be able to call such a sweet creature mine!"

Romeo heard Juliet hurrying up the walk. "It is so good to see you again, my love!" he cried, clasping her hands in his own.

"My love for you has grown so much that I can scarcely hold it all in," Juliet told him.

"Come," Friar Laurence said, smiling at them fondly. "Let us make you man and wife."

Things are going great now that Romeo and Juliet are married. But methinks there may be trouble ahead. What could possibly go wrong?

12
Death in the Square

Shortly after Romeo and Juliet finished their wedding vows, our story takes us back to the town square. A group of Montagues are on one side, and a group of Capulets are on the other. Need I say more?

As Benvolio and Mercutio sat in the town square, Benvolio began to get a little nervous. "Maybe we should get out of here, Mercutio," he said. "There's a whole gang of Capulets down the road. We really don't want to get into a fight again."

Unfortunately it was too late to avoid the Capulets. When Benvolio looked up, he found over a dozen Capulets standing before them.

"Uh-oh," gasped Benvolio in a whisper. "It's the Capulets."

"Ho-ho!" bellowed Mercutio. "It's the idiots."

Tybalt, who stood in the center of the group, took a step forward and spoke. "I'd like a word with one of you," he said coldly.

"Just one word?" asked Mercutio. "Why not a word and a punch in the face?"

"I would be glad to deal with you in that way," answered Tybalt sternly, "if you should ever give me reason to."

"I have to give you a reason?" mocked Mercutio.

"Mercutio," continued Tybalt, who was in no mood for jokes, "I know you often speak with Romeo."

"I've had enough of speaking to you," Mercutio said. "So if you want to keep speaking, say hello to Mister Sword."

As Mercutio drew his sword, Benvolio pushed it away. "You two shouldn't be fighting here in front of everyone," he warned. "Why don't you step aside and talk things over quietly? The Prince's officers have been passing through every ten minutes, and people are stopping to look!"

"Let them look," said Mercutio, taking a step closer to Tybalt and clutching his sword. "I'm not budging."

Tybalt and Mercutio stared into one another's eyes for a moment. Then Tybalt noticed Romeo approaching through the square.

"I'll deal with you some other time," Tybalt muttered. "Here's the man I want to fight."

As Tybalt and his Capulet gang moved toward Romeo, Mercutio and Benvolio followed along. Tybalt walked right up to Romeo and barked in his face. "Romeo, you invaded my family's feast and broke into our very home. You're a filthy criminal and a piece of scum!"

A month ago, even a week ago, Romeo might have been enraged by Tybalt's insult. He might have spit in his face, shoved him, or even drawn his sword. But now Romeo was a changed man. Tybalt waited for the anger to appear in Romeo's gaze. So did the other Capulets. So did Mercutio and Benvolio. But no trace of anger appeared on Romeo's face. If anything, there was only grief—even pity.

"Tybalt," Romeo finally spoke, "I will ignore your anger." Romeo started to walk away, but Tybalt followed him, stunned.

"You're looking for someone to get angry at you, but I'm not about to," Romeo continued. "Good-bye."

Tybalt wasn't going to let Romeo get away that easily. He signaled his friends to surround Romeo. Then Tybalt stepped forward and tried to provoke him once again. "By invading our party, you humiliated my entire family. So draw your sword this instant!"

But Romeo remained just as calm as before. "I never meant to hurt you in any way. In fact, I love you as though you were my own relative." Tybalt really was Romeo's relative now, but of course, Romeo had to keep that a secret. "And so, good Capulet, since I love your family's name as much as I love my own, please let us part in peace."

Tybalt was shocked. So was Mercutio. "You fool!" Mercutio cried out as Romeo walked away. "You're giving up a fight that could be easily won!"

Tybalt grinned at his friends, proud of his triumph. But his moment of glory was interrupted by Mercutio. "Excuse me, Mister Rat. I hope you're not planning to scurry back to the filthy gutter you call home."

"What do you want from me?" Tybalt shot back.

"Nothing," Mercutio responded.

Tybalt turned to depart with his friends. Then he heard the rest of Mercutio's answer. "Nothing except your worthless little life."

"That does it," Tybalt barked, drawing his sword.

At once the other Capulets backed away to give Mercutio and Tybalt room for their duel. Each pointed his long slender sword at the other, circling each other, waiting for just the right moment to strike.

"Come on, Mercutio," Romeo called. "You know the Prince forbids fighting in the streets."

Ignoring Romeo's warning, Mercutio shouted at his opponent. "Let's go, Tybalt the Terrible. Come on, Capulet. Let's see if you're worth your pretty little cap, Cap-ulet. Capu-let me see what you're made of!" With this taunt, Mercutio lunged toward Tybalt. Tybalt backed off a step, then lunged right back at Mercutio.

The two smacked their blades together swiftly, the rapid clicking of the metal pounding out a frantic melody. A crowd of Capulets and Montagues surrounded them, drifting first in one direction, then the next, as the fighters shifted positions.

"Beat down their weapons!" Romeo screamed. "Someone's going to get hurt. Isn't anyone going to do anything?"

But no one responded to Romeo's cry for peace. No one wanted peace. They coached the fighters, laughing and cheering them on. Clearly, no one was about to stop this forbidden fight.

"Please, Tybalt," persisted Romeo. "Mercutio, stop!" Romeo watched helplessly as his friend and his new cousin thrust their deadly weapons at each other's face and chest.

As his disgust grew, Romeo decided it was time to do something drastic. He decided to put his own life on the line to end their deadly fight.

So Romeo jumped between the fighters with his arms outstretched. For a moment it seemed like a perfect idea. Neither fighter could see the other! Romeo pushed Mercutio's blade aside and went to embrace him.

But Romeo's attempt to make peace backfired. As he held Mercutio, Tybalt's sword slipped under Romeo's arm—straight into Mercutio's heart.

13

The Battle Continues

The bitter hatred between the Montagues and the Capulets has turned deadly once again.

"Mercutio's been stabbed!" someone in the crowd shouted. A chill ran through Romeo's body. His friend hung limp in his arms. As he laid Mercutio down, Romeo saw blood trickling from his chest.

"Ouch," Mercutio said softly, still joking even as he lost his strength.

"Someone send for a doctor!" Benvolio cried, though he could tell it was too late.

"You're hurt," gasped Romeo.

"It's just a scratch," joked Mercutio, writhing in pain on the ground.

"Try to be brave," Romeo urged him. "A doctor's on the way. The wound doesn't look that big."

"Oh no, it's not that big," Mercutio said. "It's not as big as a door, or as deep as the sea. But it'll do the trick. Come looking for me tomorrow, and you'll find me a grave man."

For once, no one was laughing at Mercutio. Everyone realized these jokes would be his last.

"I'm finished. Done for. Over. This is the end of Mercutio," he gasped. Then he dropped the act and let his anger show. "The nerve!" he squealed. "What kind of cat would scratch a man to death? What stinking rat? What lying, stinking..." Then he looked straight at Romeo. "Why did you get between us? I was killed under your arm."

"I—I...thought it would be for the best...." Romeo hated his apology even as the words came out of his mouth.

In the play, one of Mercutio's last lines is: "A plague o' both your houses!" He curses both the Capulets and the Montagues. This character, who had been so funny, dies a very angry man.

Mercutio curled up in pain and cried out with a last burst of strength. He twisted and gasped for a moment. Then he lay still.

"Oh Romeo," Benvolio wailed. "Our friend Mercutio is dead."

Romeo hardly heard Benvolio's words. He was filled with anger—mostly at himself. "My dear friend, killed by the man who came looking for *me*," he thought. "My love for Juliet has made me a weakling. A coward."

As Romeo looked up, he saw that Tybalt had returned. He saw his friend's murderer, and his anger ripped right through him, blasting away understanding, forgiveness, and love. It even pushed the image of his dear wife from his mind. This wasn't his wife's cousin he was facing. This was his bitter enemy.

"Now, Tybalt," Romeo shouted, rising to his feet, "you wanted a fight with Romeo? Here he is!"

Tybalt backed off. "Don't run, you coward," Romeo called after him. "Mercutio has stopped on his way to heaven. He's waiting for you to keep him company."

Getting Tybalt to fight was never very hard. The spark of Romeo's rage ignited the fire in Tybalt's heart that had briefly died down. He drew his bloody blade, and pointed it at Romeo.

Romeo charged straight at Tybalt like a crazed animal. He knocked Tybalt's blade aside with his arm and pushed his enemy against a stone wall. Tybalt caught his breath and spit in Romeo's face. The two rolled in the dusty street like madmen.

Tybalt staggered to his feet and started to run away, but Romeo grabbed his legs and dragged him back. The two tumbled into a fountain, sending the birds that had been perched there scattering in all directions.

Romeo leaped out of the fountain and wiped

water from his eyes. He lost sight of Tybalt. Then he caught a glimpse of Benvolio pointing across the plaza.

Suddenly Romeo saw Tybalt picking up his fallen sword and running straight toward him.

Romeo searched the plaza frantically for his sword. Finally he spotted it lying near the fountain. He snatched up his weapon in his sweating hand and turned to see Tybalt lunging at him at full speed. Hardly thinking, Romeo held out his blade. Tybalt ran right onto it and then fell to the ground—dead.

Romeo released his grip and let his sword fall. "What have you done, Romeo?" howled Benvolio. "Run! Now! People saw you. They've called the Prince's officers. The Prince is on his way!"

"The Prince?" Romeo exclaimed. He stood still for a second, remembering how the Prince had planned to punish those who broke the peace. Then he began to run.

Within minutes, members of both families began pouring into the square. The Capulets were horrified to find Tybalt slain. The Montagues were furious to learn that Tybalt had murdered their dear Mercutio.

Then the Prince galloped into the square. As he heard the story of what had happened, he became angry. Only days before, he'd warned both families to put an end to this violence at all costs. And they hadn't listened.

Clearly, he had to make an example of the wrongdoers. He had to see that they were punished.

The young man who killed Mercutio had already been punished; Tybalt lay dead. But the man who murdered Tybalt had to be punished as well. So the Prince proclaimed a punishment for Romeo—banishment.

14
Bad News

Sometimes when Shakespeare's characters are alone, they share their thoughts with the audience by delivering monologues called soliloquies. A soliloquy is a monologue a character speaks when there's no one else on stage. At this point in the play, Juliet delivers a soliloquy, thinking out loud about how hard it is to wait for important news.

"Why is my Nurse so slow?" thought Juliet as she darted around in her bedroom like a caged deer. "It's been half an hour since I sent her to find out if my husband would be able to meet me tonight. She's probably gabbing with everyone she sees. Why doesn't she just run home to bring me news from my Romeo?"

Juliet plopped down onto her bed and lay on her back. Then she smiled and curled up into a ball, hugging her knees tightly to her chest. She felt sure Romeo would come after dark. He always seemed to find a way. "If only day would hurry up and end, so it could be night already!" she whispered to herself. "I've just got to see Romeo tonight, and tomorrow night, and the next night, and every single night for as long as I live."

Juliet smiled at the thought. Then she grew impatient again. "What in the world could be keeping my Nurse?" she muttered aloud. "If she were on crutches, she could have found him and returned by now."

Juliet rolled onto her stomach and pounded her pillow. "What a stupid situation I'm stuck in," she brooded. "I'm married, but I can't even be seen in public with my husband!"

Finally Juliet heard the Nurse's footsteps on the stairs outside her door, along with her familiar huffing and puffing. But when Juliet ran to greet her messenger, she was puzzled by the redness in her eyes. Clearly the Nurse had been crying.

"He's dead!" the Nurse wailed. "He's dead, Juliet. What ever will we do? He's dead, dead and gone."

"My Romeo...my husband...dead?" Juliet gasped. "Can luck be so awful?"

"Luck can be awful," said the Nurse. "And so can Romeo. Oh lady, what will we do?"

"Hurry up and tell me what you mean, Nurse!" Juliet demanded as the Nurse sank into a chair, weeping. "Is Romeo dead? Is he gone?"

"I saw the wound with my own eyes," the Nurse wailed.

"My life is over," gasped Juliet.

"Oh Tybalt, Tybalt!" cried the Nurse. "The best friend I ever had, and the finest man I knew. I never dreamed I'd live to see him dead."

"What?" Juliet asked. "Is Tybalt dead, and Romeo too? My cousin *and* my husband?"

"Tybalt's been killed in a duel, my lady," said the Nurse, finally pulling herself together enough to explain. "And Romeo, who killed him, has been banished from Verona forever."

"Romeo is alive? Romeo killed Tybalt?" Juliet asked in disbelief.

As the Nurse sobbed, love and hate battled in Juliet's heart. On the one hand, Romeo was her husband, and he had only been kind and gentle to her. On the other, her cousin was dead by Romeo's hand! "How could someone be so different from what they seem?" she wondered aloud. "A sweet murderer?"

Juliet paused for a moment and tried to relax. But then her heart was broken by a single word the Nurse had said. "Banished?" she asked. "My husband, chased from Verona forever? That one word is worse than Tybalt dying a thousand times!"

Juliet seized her Nurse by the shoulders and demanded details. Could the Prince's mind be changed? Could the punishment be delayed?

The Nurse's words offered little comfort. "The Prince refuses to be swayed, Juliet. If Romeo is found in Verona after dawn tomorrow, that day will be his last."

Hearing this, Juliet broke into a hysterical fit of weeping. Would she ever be able to see her husband again? Finally Juliet collected herself enough to ask the Nurse to invite Romeo to visit her that night before he had to leave Verona forever. Juliet just had to see her dear husband one last time.

Romeo has been banished? It's just one problem after another for Romeo and Juliet. First, their families kept them apart. Now the law is keeping them apart too. As Shakespeare himself said in another play, "The course of true love never did run smooth!"

15
Banished

Now let's join Romeo, who has gone to see the Friar. He's about to hear how the Prince has punished him for Tybalt's death.

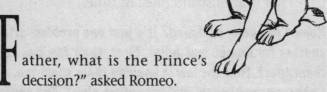

"Father, what is the Prince's decision?" asked Romeo.

"You are fortunate. It is not death, but banishment," said the Friar.

"Banished?" shrieked Romeo. "I'd rather be dead!"

The Friar charged across the floor of his study. "You rude, ungrateful boy!" the Friar scolded. "The Prince had vowed to punish such bloody deeds as yours by death. But he took pity on you and changed that frightful word *death* to *banishment*. This is mercy! Kindness! A generous gift! And you don't even appreciate it!"

"It's torture, not mercy," Romeo wailed. "Life is in Verona, where Juliet lives."

"Listen to reason," the Friar demanded, trying to lift Romeo up off the floor.

"What good is reason?" Romeo shouted. "Reason can't make a Juliet. Or move Verona someplace else. Or change a single thing that's happened. So don't bore me with reason."

"Tybalt would have killed you, but you killed Tybalt," the Friar reasoned, "so you escaped death once. The Prince might have had you killed, but he decided not to, so you escaped death a second time. Your life has been spared twice in one day!"

Even as the Friar spoke, Romeo's wailing became louder. Suddenly his crying was interrupted by a pounding at the door of the Friar's study. "Hide!" the Friar gasped. "They're coming to get you!" Romeo leaped to his feet and staggered about, searching for a place to hide.

But the friendly voice that called through the door ended his search. "I come from Juliet!" called the Nurse.

"Does Juliet think that I'm an awful murderer?" Romeo asked as soon as the Nurse entered the room. "Has she sworn never to see me again? What does she say about me?"

The Nurse explained that Juliet had forgiven Romeo for killing Tybalt. Romeo calmed down a little and listened to the Friar's plan.

The Friar explained that he knew a place Romeo could stay in the nearby town of Mantua. Romeo should obey the Prince's decree, leave town, and stay in

Mantua—for a while. Meanwhile, when the time was right, the Friar would let everyone know about Romeo's marriage to Juliet, and beg the Prince to forgive Romeo and let him back into town to live with his wife. "If you can only be patient, my son," the Friar insisted, "I'm sure that someday soon I'll be able to summon you back to Verona. I'll send you news of Juliet every day until then, so you can hear how she's doing."

The Friar's words gave Romeo hope. And the Nurse's words thrilled him even more when she told him of Juliet's invitation to visit her that night.

But even as Romeo wiped the tears from his face and prepared to meet his love, another young man was on his way to the Capulets' house to visit the beautiful Juliet.

Another young guy? Could it possibly be Paris, the Italian count with the fancy clothes and nice hair? Is he still trying to get Juliet to marry him, even though she's already married? Ah, but Paris doesn't know that!

16

Sad Farewell

In Shakespeare's day, they didn't use big set pieces—like bedroom walls, or castle doors, or rows of trees—to show you where a scene was taking place on the stage. So sometimes Shakespeare gave his characters lines that made it clear where the action was taking place. At this point in the play, for example, as Lord Capulet enters, he explains to Paris that Juliet is upstairs in bed. This tells the audience that the action has moved from the Friar's church to the Capulets' house. Because Shakespeare built this information into the lines, you don't need lots of complicated set pieces to do Shakespeare's plays nowadays. In fact, you can even do them in an empty space, like a park!

"Juliet's in no condition to come down to see you right now," Lord Capulet explained to Count Paris. "She loved her cousin Tybalt dearly and has been miserable ever since she heard of his death."

Paris was clearly disappointed, but Capulet had made up his mind. "Besides, it's very late!" he explained. "If you hadn't paid us this sudden visit, I'd be in bed myself."

"I'm sorry to have troubled you, sir," replied Paris. "Please tell your daughter how truly sorry I am to hear the tragic news."

"We will," Lady Capulet assured him. "And we'll get an answer to your question about marriage."

"I'll tell her what a fine young man you are," Capulet added, "and strongly encourage her to accept your offer. I think she'll do as I ask. In fact, I'm positive. She's such a good, obedient girl."

Paris was thrilled. "Did you want to marry her Wednesday?" Capulet asked. "Let's see, today's Monday. Wednesday's too soon! You can wait until Thursday, can't you?"

"Certainly, sir!" Paris exclaimed, as his heart leaped.

The more Capulet thought about the idea of marriage, the more he liked it. "Go tell Juliet the news, wife," he commanded. "It won't be a large ceremony, with Tybalt's recent death. Only a dozen friends or so. But how it will cheer poor Juliet!"

I hope old Lord Capulet has a good, sturdy roof on his home. Because when Juliet finds out his plans for her

marriage to Paris, she might just go straight through it! (The roof, I mean.)

"I wish that Thursday were tomorrow!" said Paris as he hurried out.

Later, Romeo left the Friar's and slipped into Juliet's room. The two hugged one another with all their might. "You don't really have to leave so soon, do you?" Juliet implored. "It won't be day for hours. That chirping you hear is the nightingale, who sings in the middle of the night. It's not the lark, who chirps when it's almost dawn."

But it was the lark, as they both well knew. Soon the first streaks of dawn would wash across the sky. "I must be gone and live, or stay and die," Romeo whispered in Juliet's ear.

"That streak isn't daylight," Juliet insisted. "It's a meteor that was sent to light your way to Mantua. You don't have to leave me yet."

Though Romeo knew the time had come to go, he couldn't move. How could he leave Juliet? He belonged with her! He tore himself away and took a step back to the balcony. Then he rushed back to Juliet and squeezed her tightly.

Suddenly Juliet remembered the Prince's threat. "Go! Go!" she urged Romeo, hurrying him to his feet. "It will be morning soon, and you've got to get out of town—or else!"

As Romeo climbed onto the branch outside Juliet's window, they heard a frantic knocking on the door to her bedroom. "Your mother's on the way up to talk to you!" warned the Nurse.

"I'd better hear from you every day," Juliet whispered. "No, every hour! Because every hour, every minute feels like a day when I'm not with you."

"I'll be thinking of you every second," Romeo replied, sliding down the branch.

As Romeo landed softly on the ground, Juliet called down to him, "Do you think we'll ever see each other again?"

Romeo stared up at Juliet in silence, as if memorizing every detail of her face. A rush of memories filled his mind. It was only two days ago he stood in that very spot, saying good-bye to her for the first time. "I'm sure we will," he assured her. "And someday we'll look back on these hard times and smile."

After Juliet watched her husband disappear in the distance, she fell back onto her bed. Though Romeo had assured her all would be well, she shivered with fear. Deep in her stomach she felt a strange, awful dread that she'd never see Romeo again. "They say the wheel of fortune is always turning around and around," she thought. "It brings good luck, then bad luck, then good luck again, as it spins and spins. Well, it had better keep turning, because my luck is terrible right now."

Suddenly the door to her room swung open. Her mother entered, bringing news that she thought would bring her daughter the good fortune she deserved. At least, that's what the news was intended to do....

How in the world did Shakespeare ever keep track of all the little twists and turns in this story? It must have been as fun for him to write this play as it is for us to read it. Which reminds me...turn the page!

17
Marriage—Or Else

Lady Capulet finds Juliet crying. She thinks Juliet is upset over Tybalt's death. But we know she is upset over Romeo's banishment. That's why their conversation may seem a little strange....

"**Y**ou must stop weeping for your cousin," Lady Capulet urged her daughter. "No matter how many tears you cry, you can't make him live again."

Of course, Juliet wasn't crying for Tybalt, but for the loss of her husband. That's why her mother's next remark took Juliet completely by surprise. "I think your tears aren't because of Tybalt's death, but because of Romeo."

"What do you mean, Mother?" Juliet asked, alarmed.

"You cry because you're angry that the murderer still lives," Lady Capulet explained.

"You're right, Mother," Juliet answered. "I cry because that man lives far from me. If only he were here right now! I'd take matters into my own hands!"

"Well spoken, Juliet," answered her mother, believing Juliet's feelings for Romeo to be the opposite of what they really were. "But enough about Romeo. We have some good news to discuss."

As Juliet's mother explained that she was to marry Paris on Thursday morning, Juliet's mind was filled with disgust and rage. Had the news come at another time, she would have answered politely. But since she was already miserable about saying good-bye to Romeo, Juliet couldn't take any more. So she exploded. "Why should I marry Paris? I don't even know him!" she shrieked. "I'd rather marry Romeo— whom you know I hate—than Paris!"

At the same time, Juliet's father was making his way up the stairs. He couldn't wait to see how happy his plan would make Juliet. The chance to be married to such a popular young gentleman was every girl's dream!

When Lord Capulet entered the room and saw Juliet's face covered with tears, his heart sank. How much pain the poor girl felt over the loss of her cousin. Hadn't his wife told Juliet about the marriage yet? Surely that would chase away those tears. Why wouldn't Lady Capulet hurry up and announce the good news?

"I've already told her," Lady Capulet answered. "She says she won't have him."

Capulet could hardly believe what he was hearing. "You don't count yourself lucky to have so worthy a man as Paris?" he asked.

"No, I don't feel lucky at all," Juliet answered curtly. "I'm grateful that you tried to please me. But the way you've gone about it doesn't please me in the least. So thank you. But no thank you."

In an instant, all of Capulet's tender feelings for his daughter changed to anger. "What's this?" he roared. "You thank me, but you don't thank me? Well, keep your thanks to yourself. And get ready to be married on Thursday morning, you ungrateful child."

Juliet fell to her knees and begged her father to change his mind. But he was far beyond the point of listening to anyone. Each pleading word from Juliet only rubbed more salt into the wound. "Get yourself to church on Thursday or never look me in the face again," he raged.

Juliet was crushed by these words. When the Nurse heard Juliet crying, she burst in and demanded that Lord Capulet stop shouting at her. But the Nurse's plea was useless too, and only made Lord Capulet shout louder. "Hold your tongue, you old gossip!" he screamed at the Nurse.

When his wife tried to calm him, Capulet yelled at her too. "Every hour since she was born, all I ever thought about was this child," he ranted. "I bought her the best of everything. I gave her everything she needed. I worried about her every minute of every day, all so that someday she would marry well. And now this Paris—the perfect man, a man with everything one could ask for—comes along, and she won't have him? She says, 'No thank you, Father! But excuse me, Father!' Well, you listen to me, young lady. If you don't marry Paris, I'll excuse you, all right. I'll excuse you from this house forever. Do as you like, you won't be my daughter any more."

After her father stormed out, Juliet pleaded with her mother to speak to him, to delay the marriage even a week. But her mother had no interest in provoking her husband any further. She left the room, urging Juliet to do as he said.

Only the Nurse stayed behind to comfort Juliet, but her advice was not very cheerful. "Listen, my dear," the Nurse began. "Romeo's gone, far away. You might never see him again. Even if you do, it will have to be in little bits of time, since he'll have to sneak around. But Count Paris is a wonderful gentleman. He's rich, handsome, and better looking than Romeo, if you ask me! If I were you, I'd marry him."

"You're no help," muttered Juliet. For the first time, Juliet felt completely alone. Even the Nurse wasn't on her side anymore. "Tell my mother I'll think about the marriage," she requested. "I'm going to see Friar Laurence to make confession for upsetting my father."

The Nurse thought that Juliet was beginning to accept the idea of marrying Paris. But Juliet hadn't changed her mind at all. Romeo was her husband and her true love, and nothing anyone could say or do would change that. Her plan was to see the Friar to ask for his advice. The thought of marrying Paris after already being married to Romeo was unthinkable.

Hoping the Friar would have an answer to her problem, Juliet left for the monastery.

18

A Dangerous Plan

While Juliet is on her way to see the Friar to ask for his help, Paris is already there discussing his wedding plans. Juliet sees Paris, and she has to act like she's really going to marry him. But we know better, don't we?

"How lucky I am to run into my bride!" said Paris as Juliet charged into the Friar's study. Paris had dropped in on the Friar to ask him to perform the wedding on Thursday. As Juliet came face to face with the man who was the cause of her latest problems, she was at a loss for words.

"I will be your bride..." she said, "when I can be a bride."

"You *will* be a bride on Thursday," Paris replied.

"What will be, will be," Juliet answered back, glancing at the Friar.

"That's true, indeed," the Friar answered.

After an awkward silence, Paris asked, "So have you come to make confession to the Friar?"

"If I answered that, I'd be confessing to you," Juliet answered, wishing Paris would leave her in peace.

Paris took Juliet's nervous glances around the room as a sign that she was feeling shy about being near her husband-to-be. "Anyway, I'll see you on Thursday," he said. "Until then, take this kiss." He kissed Juliet's frozen lips, then departed.

After that difficult meeting, Juliet was exhausted...and desperate for a plan. The Friar came up with a plan quickly. But it was a risky plan that depended on perfect timing and would take tremendous courage on Juliet's part.

Gesturing that Juliet should follow, the Friar led Juliet down a set of stairs to a room in the basement of the church. A strange blend of smells filled the room. Without speaking, the Friar got right to work at a table in the center of the room. With great care, he selected a few leaves from each of four different jugs and laid them on his table. Then he went over to a shelf, stepped onto a footstool, and pulled out a tiny box that rested on top. Inside the box was the small purple flower that had a sweet smell. The Friar placed a petal from this flower with the other leaves on the table, pounded them together, and mixed them with an acid in a vial.

Then he put a cork in the vial, handed it to Juliet, and finally spoke. "Go home," he said. "Tell your father you'll marry Paris. Then, on Wednesday night, drink this potion. Every drop."

Juliet nodded silently. The Friar continued, "Your heart will appear to stop beating. The blood will appear to stop moving through your veins. You won't blink, or twitch, or even breathe. Your cheeks will become pale and your eyes will fall shut. You'll appear so much like a corpse that not even a doctor will know you're alive. When they come to wake you for the wedding, everyone will believe you're dead. They'll take you to the Capulet family vault in the cemetery—that big stone house where the bodies of all your dead relatives lie."

Juliet didn't care for the idea of lying alongside the bodies of her relatives who'd been dead for years...or alongside the mangled body of Tybalt, who'd only recently been laid there. But the Friar explained how this trick would lead her to freedom. "In the meantime," he continued, "I'll send for Romeo and let him know of our plan. He'll arrive at the tomb before the potion wears off. You'll awaken as if from a pleasant sleep, and Romeo will take you away to Mantua."

Juliet took the potion from the Friar's hand and said, "Love will give me strength." As he bid her farewell, the Friar did his best to assure her all would be well. But as he closed the door behind her, his smile faded. He sank into his chair and slumped forward. So many things had gone wrong for this young couple. At this point there was no room for error.

No wonder the Friar's nervous. Every time he makes a plan, something messes it up! He marries Romeo & Juliet to bring peace, and Romeo is banished. He sends Romeo to Mantua to lay low, and Juliet is being forced to marry Paris. I hope this plan with the potion will work.

19

Potion of Death

Now Lord Capulet is planning to put on a really big celebration in honor of Juliet's marriage to Paris—an even fancier party than the one he threw earlier in the story. But I have a feeling this party isn't going to go exactly as planned.

Juliet's father was thrilled. "What a wonderful Friar!" he said cheerfully. "What an amazing man he is to have convinced you that you were wrong. And so quickly!" As soon as Juliet had announced her decision to go along with the wedding, her father began pushing ahead with plans for the celebration as fast as he could. After all, it was only a couple of days away! He hired extra cooks so the kitchen would be bustling round the clock. He hired a tailor to prepare the finest gowns for the his daughter and wife. And he hired three different troupes of musicians. At a celebration this special, the dancing must never stop.

Somehow Juliet managed to convince everyone that she really was willing to marry Paris. Her mother had no idea that she was pretending. The servants couldn't tell. Not even the Nurse suspected that Juliet was hiding anything, though she did notice Juliet was often deep in thought.

Then came the night before the wedding, the time for the Friar's plan to go into action. Juliet locked her door, went to her cabinet, opened the bottom drawer, and fished around until she found a certain red stocking. Then she went to her bed, reached into the stocking, and pulled out the little vial the Friar had given her.

Outside her door Juliet heard her father hurrying from one part of the house to the other, attending to every last detail so everything would be ready by dawn.

She stared at the purple liquid in the bottle. When Juliet had first heard the plan, drinking the potion sounded easy. But she was having second thoughts. She didn't like the idea of drinking something that would make her heart appear to stop beating.

As Juliet squeezed the vial containing the potion, her fingertips turned cold. She was scared. "Suppose the Friar didn't mix this right and I never wake up," she wondered. "Or suppose it's a poison that the Friar made to get rid of me, so that no one would find out he married me in secret. No, he wouldn't do that. But suppose I wake up too early. What then?" Her imagination began to race. "I'll be gasping for air, locked in the tomb with the corpses of all my dead grandparents. Their ghosts may rise up, shrieking and howling all around me."

Just then she heard another sound downstairs. Her father wasn't alone any more. He was speaking with someone. Food had arrived. Musicians were setting up. It was time to choose: she must either drink this liquid now, or marry Paris.

Juliet removed the cork and whispered, "Romeo, I drink to you." She opened her lips and poured the liquid down her throat.

I sure hope that stuff works. And quickly!

20
A Horrible Discovery

So far, so good. The plan seems to be working. Let's see what happens when the Nurse tries to wake Juliet from her "sleep."

"Wake up, mistress!" called the Nurse, approaching the bed upon which the bride-to-be lay still. "Fast asleep, I see. Deep in a sweet dream about her new love, I bet," she thought. "Come on, sleepyhead. Rise and shine!"

As the Nurse took out Juliet's wedding clothing, she continued to chatter away merrily. She joked and teased, and told stories of her own wedding day.

Then the Nurse noticed something strange. Juliet wasn't in her bedclothes. She was dressed in the clothes she'd worn the night before. And she wasn't moving at all.

The Nurse shook Juliet's body. Then she shook it again, and again. But it was still. Completely still. Her mistress wasn't sleeping. Her mistress wasn't stalling. Her mistress appeared to be dead.

Seconds later the Nurse began to shriek! Juliet's father and mother rushed into the room. Old Capulet touched Juliet's palm. It was cold. He pressed the vein in her wrist for her pulse. There was none. He put his palm to her mouth. No breath came. "Dead!" he gasped as he collapsed to the floor.

Paris arrived to join Juliet's parents and Nurse in grieving. How angry they all felt, as though death had robbed them of the thing they loved most in the world.

But the next person to arrive wasn't angry at all. In fact, at the sight of Juliet's lifeless body, he breathed a sigh of relief. It was the Friar, who had been summoned to perform the wedding ceremony. He was relieved to see that Juliet had been brave enough to use his potion—and that it seemed to be doing its job.

"Why do you weep, to know that she is in heaven?" Friar Laurence began. He had to do his best to console the mourners as quickly as he could so they could hurry up and get her to the tomb. "All your lives you wished the best for her. So you must not mourn now that she has achieved the best: eternal life in heaven."

When he finished his brief sermon, the Friar saw to it that Juliet was carried to the tomb carefully and gently. As he left the Capulets' grounds, his heart raced. So far his plan was moving along smoothly. He had already sent a message to Romeo; a messenger who had been planning to pass through Mantua carried the letter. Any minute now, Romeo would be thrilled to learn that it was time to come for Juliet.

But the Friar's message wasn't the only thing traveling quickly along. So was a piece of bad news from Verona. The news of Juliet's death on her wedding morning spread like wildfire in all directions. It spread all through Verona. And it spread beyond Verona into neighboring towns. It even spread into the little town of Mantua.

That's where Romeo is! Yet another plot twist. Two pieces of news are headed Romeo's way: a message from Friar Laurence explaining that Juliet's death is a hoax, and a message that Juliet has died! Which message will Romeo get first?

21

Romeo Finds Out

Unfortunately the news that reached Romeo first was about the death of Juliet. What will he do now that he thinks Juliet is dead?

No one who happened to pass Romeo as he walked along the streets of Mantua that afternoon suspected that anything in particular was on his mind. His pace was relaxed. His steps were even. He stared ahead. His face displayed no emotion at all.

As Romeo passed by an inn where he'd eaten lunch the day before, a groundskeeper waved. But Romeo just kept on walking ahead, seeming not to notice.

He walked down one road, turned sharply down another, and then turned down a narrow alley. Finally he arrived at a small rundown store. He passed straight by the shelves, not noticing the boxes, pots, bottles, spools of thread, and other things on display. Romeo went directly to the back of the shop, where the shop owner stood behind a counter that was covered with small bottles.

"What will it be, sir?" asked the owner. "My new shampoo from the Orient? A serum guaranteed to cure a cold, help you sleep, and keep your toes warm on a winter night?" Romeo just stood there silently. "Perfume for a sweetheart? This one will win her heart, for sure, made from crushed roses, it is! Speak up, my silent friend. I can't read your mind, you know!"

But as the shop owner studied Romeo's blank expression, he sensed some frightful plot brewing behind this young man's eyes. He realized exactly what Romeo wanted. "Sorry, friend," he said, lowering his voice. "I don't have any of that stuff. It's against the law."

Romeo reached into the small money bag that hung at his side, pulled out three gold coins, and placed them down on the counter. "I guess you didn't hear me," the shop owner said. "I don't have any. And even if I did, I couldn't sell it to you. They could hang me for selling it."

Again Romeo reached into his money bag. This time he pulled out another coin, and another, and another, until the sack was empty. The man stared at the small pile of gold coins that lay before him. He could live half a year on that much money!

When Romeo departed from the shop, his money bag held the small bottle of black liquid that he'd purchased. The liquid was poison.

• • • • •

As the sun began to set over Verona, a messenger returned to town on horseback. He was anxious to return home and get some sleep after his exhausting journey. But first, he knew he had to visit someone.

"Romeo must have been pleased by my message," Friar Laurence said to the messenger as he welcomed him into his office.

"I had to take a different route this time," the messenger explained. "There was a town along the highway where everyone had the plague, so I couldn't pass through. I had to take a detour around Mantua, and wasn't able to deliver your letter. I could return it to you now, or I can deliver it on my journey next week—"

"You didn't deliver my message?" Friar Laurence was horrified. Juliet would awaken in less than an hour, and Romeo hadn't been summoned to take her from the tomb. All of the Friar's carefully laid plans were coming undone.

In a flash Friar Laurence decided to break into the tomb himself, rescue Juliet, and hide her in the church. If he didn't hurry across town to the cemetery, this plan would be just as much a failure as all his others. Juliet would wake up alone, trapped in an airtight tomb—and gasp for air, helpless, as she suffocated to death.

Meanwhile, Paris stood holding a bouquet of flowers outside the tomb where Juliet's body lay.

"How I hoped to scatter these flowers on our bridal bed," he said. "But instead, I can only scatter them by the bed where you now rest in death. Tonight I leave them here for you, fair Juliet, as I will every night until I die."

Suddenly Paris froze. He wasn't alone. He heard footsteps on the dry grass, and saw a shadowy shape moving closer in the darkness. The shape just stood there between a pair of tombstones, staring right at him. Paris squinted at the shape for a moment. Then he realized that it was Romeo.

Will Romeo and Paris have a showdown in the graveyard? It's this kind of suspense that makes my fur stand straight up!

22

Death in the Graveyard

"Are you still angry at the poor Capulet family?" Paris shouted at Romeo. "First you murder Tybalt. Then, on the night of Juliet's funeral, you come to smash their tomb with that iron bar?"

Romeo was indeed carrying a long, curved iron bar that he'd brought from Mantua. But he hadn't come to smash the tomb. He'd come to open it. After hearing of Juliet's death, Romeo planned to see the body of his wife one last time, then end his own life.

"Don't take one step closer to that tomb, murderer!" barked Paris, reaching for his sword. "If you do, prepare to die."

"That's why I came!" answered Romeo. "To prepare to die!" Romeo took a step closer, but Paris blocked his path.

"My friend, please don't tempt me to do more violence," Romeo warned. "I mean no harm to anyone...except myself."

"I'll never let my dear love's enemy near her tomb," Paris pledged.

"Just leave me alone here for an hour," Romeo begged. "I mean no disrespect to the Capulets, and least of all to Juliet."

"No," Paris said. No matter how much Romeo pleaded with him, Paris refused to budge.

Finally Romeo gave up trying to convince Paris that he was telling the truth and marched straight toward the door of the tomb. Paris pushed him away twice. When Romeo tried to get by him again, Paris drew his sword.

It was so dark in the cemetery that the two could hardly see one another as they dueled. The moonlight provided a dull spotlight for their clumsy, desperate battle. They backed into tombstones and crashed into walls. They lost their balance and fell. Still they fought on, determined to fight to the finish.

A night watchman heard the clatter of clashing blades and saw the shadows of two frantic men. He stood still, straining his eyes to see who the fighters were.

Suddenly there was a howl of pain. The clanking stopped. The two shadows were now only one. Realizing he'd seen one man kill another, the watchman ran for help.

"Please bury me with Juliet," gasped Paris as he lay bleeding on the ground.

"I will," promised Romeo. Paris's eyes closed for the last time.

Romeo was too filled by his own sadness to grieve for his rival's death. He picked up his iron bar and made his way to the massive door of the enclosed stone house that held the Capulet dead. He wedged the curved end of the iron bar into the crevice at the edge of the door and pushed with all his might, thrusting the weight of his entire body against the long bar.

Slowly but surely, he wedged the door open. Romeo set a candle by the door and lit it, and a rich glow filled the small room. His eyes moved about the room until he saw Juliet. This was the sight Romeo had come so far to see. Romeo had sworn that wherever she went, even if she were on the farthest shore, he'd come to be by her side. And he'd made good on his promise. He had come to be with Juliet, even in her tomb.

Making good on another promise, Romeo hauled Paris's body into the tomb and rested it at the base of the slab of stone on which Juliet lay. Romeo sat down beside Juliet and took out the bottle of poison, setting it carefully on the stone beside him. Then he gazed into his sweetheart's face.

"Oh Juliet," he exclaimed. "You're so beautiful even now, even in death. Such light still pours from your cheeks that I'd almost swear you were still alive!"

He reached for the bottle.

What fate awaits our Romeo and his beloved Juliet?

23
Too Late

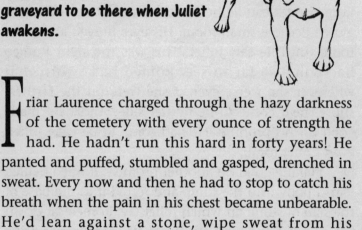

Meanwhile, the good Friar is making a mad dash for the graveyard to be there when Juliet awakens.

Friar Laurence charged through the hazy darkness of the cemetery with every ounce of strength he had. He hadn't run this hard in forty years! He panted and puffed, stumbled and gasped, drenched in sweat. Every now and then he had to stop to catch his breath when the pain in his chest became unbearable. He'd lean against a stone, wipe sweat from his forehead, and pant in loud, wheezy breaths. Then he'd be struck by the thought of Juliet waking up alone, gasping for breath in the tomb—and he'd run on.

Meanwhile people inside the Capulet house were getting worried too. A guard reported that he'd seen a murder in the cemetery near the family tomb. Another guard thought he'd heard the name Romeo shouted in the darkness. Capulet sent word to the Prince, asking for a band of officers to search the grounds.

Rumor of Romeo's return reached the Montague house as well, throwing the household into an uproar. Lord and Lady Montague called their relatives together to see what strange event was going on at the cemetery.

Though panic seized both houses, inside the Capulets' tomb all was calm. Romeo just sat there staring at Juliet. Just being near Juliet really was enough for Romeo.

"Has anyone ever been this happy just before he's about to die?" Romeo wondered to himself. "Oh, my love, my wife," he said aloud, as though she could hear him. "Death may have robbed you of life, but it hasn't taken away your beauty."

He looked over at Tybalt's body. "Well, Tybalt, now I'll give you your revenge. I'll end the life of the man who killed you. Please forgive me for what I did."

Romeo took the bottle of poison in his hand and slid off the cap. But before he drank it, he couldn't help noticing Juliet's cheeks one last time. They seemed even rosier than a few seconds ago. He couldn't believe it! "Ah, Juliet," he said aloud, "how can you still be so beautiful?"

At this point in the play Romeo says:

**"Death, that hath sucked the honey of thy breath,
Hath had no power yet upon thy beauty."**

Shakespeare has Romeo talk about Juliet's incredible beauty with incredibly beautiful words!

As he squeezed her hand, he remembered the first time he had held it at the Capulets' party. He recalled the lively music, the smells of the flowers, and the thrill of seeing her smile. How Romeo loved her! He cherished every moment they had spent together.

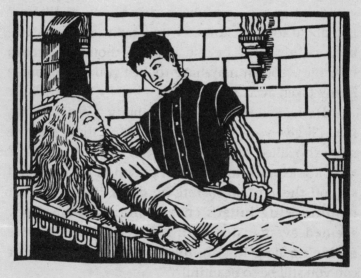

Gazing at the face of his beloved, Romeo drank down the poison. Then he kissed Juliet and rested his head on her lap. His eyes fell shut as he lay there. The only sound in the tomb was Romeo's soft, slow breathing. Then the tomb became completely silent.

As the Friar scurried around to the front of the Capulet tomb, he was thrilled. The door was open! In his haste he hadn't even thought how he'd ever open that huge stone slab. But what was it doing open? Had Juliet already awakened? Had she managed to claw her way out? Had the tomb been robbed?

And then his confusion was cleared away—and his hope was crushed. There, in the flickering light of Romeo's candle, was Romeo, his face resting on Juliet, his body hanging limp over the stone.

The Friar didn't know who told Romeo about Juliet's death. He didn't know when Romeo had returned, how he found his way to the tomb, or what thoughts had run through his mind as he ended his life. But he knew one thing for certain: Romeo was dead. The young man who'd come to him a thousand times, to question and complain, to whine and dream, had ended his own life.

As the Friar took a step closer he saw that Romeo's eyes were closed. He also saw that Juliet's eyes were open.

Juliet blinked a few times as she brought her fingers to her face. She rubbed her eyes and yawned. Here in these gloomy surroundings, Juliet looked as though she were just awakening from a sweet dream.

She smiled when she saw the Friar, and asked at once for Romeo. "Where's my love?" she asked. "How long until he gets here to take me away?"

But no sooner had Juliet spoken then she felt the head of her husband resting on her lap. "Come, Juliet," said the Friar. "A greater power than us has ruined all our plans."

"No!" Juliet gasped as she realized that Romeo was dead.

Suddenly the Friar heard people calling out in the distance—and coming closer. He jerked around, seized by panic. Suppose they found him, a holy man, trespassing in a sacred tomb? Juliet was alive and Romeo was dead, all because of his flawed scheme!

"Let's go, Juliet!" he begged, tugging her hand. "I'll drop you off at a church far away. You can become a nun. What are you waiting for?"

But Juliet wasn't about to leave the tomb where her beloved lay. The terrified Friar stumbled toward the door. "I won't stay another second," he told her as he turned and hurried off into the darkness.

Juliet was alone. She gazed down at the face of Romeo in her lap. The very first time she had seen Romeo's face, she knew she would love him always. She'd been certain of things before. As a child she knew when she wanted a certain doll, or dress, or hat. She'd love those things dearly for a while and then outgrow them. But the feeling she had for Romeo was different. It was a much deeper feeling, a truth she could always count on, like knowing that she could always look up and see the sky above her, or the ground beneath her feet. This was a friend who would always be a friend. This was her one true love. This was her husband. Juliet stroked Romeo's hair.

As Juliet sat there, she realized that she couldn't imagine her life without Romeo. She had no interest in going anywhere, or meeting anyone, or growing a day older without him.

"His dagger!" she exclaimed, noticing the small blade that gleamed in the last sparks of candlelight. She removed the dagger from Romeo's belt and held it before her chest. And then, after a moment's pause, she slipped it into her heart.

As Juliet slumped forward onto Romeo's body, she grasped his fingertips in her palm with her last ounce of strength. She twisted in pain...and then lay still. Nothing moved but their shadows, which bounced wildly across the walls as the candle flickered in a small pool of wax.

People began to arrive at the tomb: a few of the Prince's officers led by a watchman, a small group of Capulets, a group of Montague servants. Carrying torches, they crowded around the small tomb and peeked in to see what violence had occurred in the night.

Word of their findings spread through Verona in minutes. Paris was dead. Romeo was dead. Juliet was dead, but warm blood flowed from her chest as though she'd just been murdered! Swiftly, the whole town gathered upon the small plot of ground.

So did the Prince. He got down from his horse, moved to the front of the crowd, and demanded that someone tell him how all these young people had been killed.

"I can tell you," called a voice from the back of the crowd. It was Friar Laurence, trusted friend to all. He raised his wavering voice to tell the whole story of the tragedy.

"Romeo and Juliet loved one another," he began. He told of their secret love, their secret marriage, and their secret meetings. He told of the obstacles posed by Romeo's banishment and Paris's love for Juliet. He told of his desperate plot, of the potion Juliet took, and the message that was supposed to reach Romeo but never did. And he told of the night's bloody finish. "Romeo and Juliet found that their love was so great that they chose to die together rather than live apart," the Friar concluded sadly.

As the Friar finished, all stood in silence and awaited the Prince's response. "Capulet!" he called, looking into the crowd for Juliet's father. "Montague!" he called next, as Romeo's father made his way toward the Prince and stood beside Lord Capulet.

The Prince didn't know what to say. But he didn't need to say anything, because something very strange and wonderful happened.

As Juliet's father looked at his rival, he suddenly

couldn't remember why he hated him so much. The insults and injuries that he and Montague had traded over the years seemed like actions carried out by people far away, not by the two men standing there. It was as though all the hatred that had passed between their families over the generations hadn't been real, but only a game they were stuck

playing, one that had spun out of control. Capulet felt like he was awakening from a dream.

As Capulet looked into Montague's sad eyes, he didn't see an enemy. He saw a helpless man like himself, whose pointless anger had cost him the one thing he held dearest in all the world. He saw a man who had just lost his only child. Capulet didn't feel anger. He felt love. And Montague felt the same.

"If my son loved your daughter more than life itself," said Montague, "then she must have been a very precious, special person."

Capulet was silent for a moment. Then he said, "Give me your hand, friend." The two joined hands, and vowed to lay to rest the hatred between their families. Capulet announced that he would build a statue of Romeo in pure gold, and Montague offered to build one of Juliet beside it, so people far and wide would know about the great love of their two children.

And so ends the story of two young people whose great love led to violence, confusion, death— and finally, peace.

The last lines in the play, spoken by the Prince, are:

**"Never was a story of more woe
Than this of Juliet and her Romeo."**

Woe means sadness, and the story of ROMEO & JULIET is a tragedy. It doesn't have a happy ending—but a happy ending isn't always the most important thing in a story. Think about the characters. Shakespeare created characters so real that we begin to sympathize with them—in other words, we feel what they feel. We laugh when they laugh, worry when they worry, and cry when they cry. We use our imaginations to help us make the story real—and that's the most important thing.

And this little dog and his big imagination can't wait for the next good story! Until next time...see ya!

Fill Your World With WISHBONE™

WISHBONE™

Plush

Adopt a WISHBONE™
of your own.
Appearing soon as
Sherlock Holmes,
Romeo and other
legendary characters.

Video

Leap into adventure with
Wishbone℠ on home Video.
Collect all 8!

CD-ROM

"WISHBONE™ and
the Amazing Odyssey"
on CD-Rom.
http://www.palladiumnet.com

Call 1-800-888-WISH

Toll-Free number for general information.